# The Mystery of the Bermuda Triangle

**The Mystery Series**
**Book 11**

# *The Mystery of the Bermuda Triangle*

**PAUL MOXHAM**

## Copyright



www.paulmoxham.com

British English edition.

ISBN-13: 9781652261940

# CONTENTS

## CHAPTER 1

# BACK TO THE CARRIBEAN

It was a beautiful sunny day and the children were enjoying themselves on the water. Joe thought life couldn't get any better than this. He, along with his younger sisters and his best friend, were on a cabin cruiser bound for Oxley Island, an island situated on the rim of the Bermuda Triangle.

Joe wished his parents could have been with them, but something had come up and they had been unable to make it, thus the children were travelling to the island with Uti, a handsome looking man with black skin and piercing brown eyes. They had met him on their previous trip to the Caribbean and had formed a strong bond with him.

Consequently, even though Mr and Mrs Mitchell had been unable to join them on this three day excursion to one of the most remote islands in the Caribbean, they were happy to let the children go with him. The island was home to some of the rarest animals on the planet and the children had begged their parents to let them go.

As they reached the island, the sun was slowly setting. Uti tied the boat to the pier and the children then helped him unload some medical supplies, along with some cages he had brought to give to Grace, the young zoologist who was doing some research on the island.

That evening, the children accompanied their friend to the house where Grace was staying. She had prepared a huge bowl of fruit salad for them and they spent the next few hours listening to her tales about life on the island. Then, as darkness fell, and the children became tired, Uti led them back to the boat.

They had just reached the vessel when Uti suddenly paused. "Oh no! Grace gave me a package to deliver to a friend of hers and I just realised I left it back at the house. You children go aboard and I'll pop back and get it. I shouldn't be too long."

Sarah yawned. "Okay. I'm so tired, all I want to do is sleep."

Uti smiled. "Then do just that. Remember, we're going to have a big day tomorrow exploring the island from top to bottom."

Joe grinned. "I can't wait."

As Uti retreated back the way he had just come, the four children walked up the gangplank and down into the cabin. They lay down on the bunks and, in a flash, all four were fast asleep.

~

With a start, Amy suddenly awoke. As she glanced around, she wondered where she was. It then all came back to her. The Caribbean. The trip to Oxley Island. Uti going back to get the package.

Suddenly, a streak of light illuminated the night sky. As the flash lit up the cabin, Amy saw the waves crashing outside and realised a storm was raging. At the same time, she realised that the boat was rocking from side to side.

A second later, a massive clap of thunder sounded overhead. She fumbled around until she found the torch she had brought with her. As she did so, the others awoke.

“What’s going on?” Will asked.

“Why are we moving?” Sarah questioned, looking startled.

“I can’t imagine why Uti would have changed his mind about stopping at the island,” Amy replied.

“I meant to stay awake until he returned, but I must have fallen asleep before that happened.” Joe looked at his watch and was amazed to see it was almost midnight. “Gosh! We’ve been asleep for ages.”

“Let’s go and talk with Uti straight away.” Amy, holding the torch, led the way up the steps to the wheelhouse. As she flung open the door and shone the light around, she gasped out in horror. “He’s not here!”

“What? Are you sure?” Joe pushed past his sister and glanced around. She was right. There was no one in the wheelhouse.

“Do you think he’s out on deck?” Sarah asked, hopeful.

Will looked sceptical. “He’d be mad to be out there in this storm.”

As the four of them exited the wheelhouse and stepped out onto the deck, the full force of the storm hit them. The rain was pelting down and the thunder was deafening. It was the worst storm that the children had experienced for some time, especially since the boat was heaving up and down sickeningly as the waves thrust against it.

It didn’t take long for the four to ascertain that Uti wasn’t on board. Bewildered as to how this situation could have arisen, they hurried back into the wheelhouse.

"The only answer I can think of is that the storm tore the boat from its moorings before Uti returned," Will said. "If so, it's anyone's guess how long we've been drifting for."

Since it was dark, it was impossible to see if there was any land nearby. But, even so, the children spent the next few minutes peering out of the wheelhouse window, gazing out in desperation, hoping that they would see some sign of life. But, they didn't. After standing about and talking amongst themselves for a good half hour, they retreated back to the warmth of the cabin.

As they sat on the bunk beds and thought about what they could do, Amy peered through the porthole, hoping to see land. But there was none to be seen. She sighed, not knowing how they were going to get out of a situation like this. Then, suddenly, something loomed out of the darkness. "Hey, I see a boat!"

As the others crowded around her and peered through the porthole, Amy realised with horror that the boat was heading straight towards them. The bow of the oncoming vessel was going to hit them directly on their side. "Oh no, let's get out of here!"

As the others realised the danger they were in, they raced out of the cabin and up the steps to the wheelhouse.

It was fortunate that they did since, less than a minute later, there was an almighty crash and a splintering of glass and wood as the oncoming vessel smashed into the side of the cabin cruiser.

As Joe glanced back down the stairs, he saw water flooding in. He knew instantly that the cabin cruiser was doomed. It was going to sink, and sink fast. "We're sinking! We need to get out of here!"

The four children raced out of the wheelhouse and, upon reaching the railing, looked towards the boat that had hit them. It had seemed to slow down and there was a light going back and forth as though someone had a lantern. As a light suddenly lit up the children, they madly waved and called out in their loudest voices.

Within a minute, a man answered their calls for help and, shortly afterwards, a rope ladder was flung down to them. The children hurried towards it and Joe grabbed hold of it. "You girls go first!"

While the boys held the rope ladder as steady as they could, the girls clambered up. With the wind and the rain pelting their faces, it was hard work, but they did it.

As the deck of the cruiser flooded with water, Will began climbing up the ladder. Joe waited anxiously for his turn to come, glancing around him as he did so. His heart skipped a beat as he caught sight of something.

It was a wave, over ten feet tall, and headed directly for him.

## CHAPTER 2

# A FAMILIAR FACE

Joe began climbing the rope ladder as fast as his legs would take him, but he had barely gone more than a few feet before the wave smashed into him.

The massive amount of water pushed him and the ladder away from the boat and, for one awful moment, he wondered if the ladder would be torn away.

But it wasn't. Soaking wet, he slowly and surely clambered up the remaining four or five feet. He was relieved when a man reached down and pulled him up on the deck.

"Come with me," the man said, grasping Joe's shoulder.

The four followed the man along the deck and down some steps. As it was a bigger boat than the cabin cruiser, there were a number of cabins. The man told them to enter the first one on the left. He disappeared for a minute and returned with some towels and blankets so that they could dry themselves and get warm.

As the children did so, the man, who introduced himself as Spud, asked them several questions such as where were they from, what were they doing, and was anyone else aboard their boat. Once the children had answered the questions, the man nodded. "Okay, well, the boss should be along shortly. Oh, here he comes."

Spud departed and the children heard footsteps approaching. A few seconds later, a man with a long, red, bushy beard strolled in.

The children were shocked and surprised to see it was someone whom they had encountered during their last visit to the Caribbean.

It was none other than Captain Red!

"What are you kids doing here?" Captain Red exclaimed, shocked to see them.

"We could ask you the same question," Joe replied. "You're supposed to be in prison."

Captain Red chortled. "They let me out because I was a good boy."

Will shook his head. "I don't believe you. More likely you escaped."

"So what if I did?" Captain Red questioned. "What are you four going to do about it, eh?"

"Nothing," Joe said. "All we want is to go home and then—"

"And where is that?" Captain Red interrupted.

As quickly as they could, the children explained to Captain Red what had happened in the last few hours. After they had finished their story, the man stroked his beard. "Interesting. However, I'm headed for somewhere myself right now and I'm not changing course for anyone or anything. This storm is giving me a run for my money, but we'll get through it."

"But we can't go with you!" Sarah piped up.

"Let me remind you that it was my men who rescued you," Captain Red stated. "If you wish, you're free to go back to your old boat, though I doubt very much you want to since it will be at the bottom of the sea by now."

"How long will it be until you reach your destination?" Joe asked.

Captain Red shrugged his shoulders. "I can't say. It depends on the storm. But, in the meantime, just as long as you behave yourselves, I will see that you are taken care of. As much as I was annoyed and angry at you lot for losing the treasure that I found—"

"We found that treasure!" Will interrupted.

"Well, I'm sure I would have found it without you," Captain Red replied. "Anyways, as I was saying, I will treat you well just as long as you behave yourselves. I don't want you messing about in the wheelhouse and fiddling with anything, or attempting to contact someone on the radio. Just do as you're told and no harm will come to you, understand?" The man gazed at all four of the children. They all nodded. "Good. Now, I have to head back up to see how the storm is going." Captain Red exited the cabin and, after closing the door behind him, walked away.

"Gosh! That was a surprise," Joe said.

"Yes, I never expected to see Captain Red again," Will muttered.

"Do you think he got out on good behaviour?" Sarah questioned.

Joe grimly smiled. "No, I don't think so, but it doesn't matter how he got out. Even though he was a pirate and probably still is, we mustn't forget that he did rescue us."

"But that's because his boat slammed into ours!" Amy exclaimed.

Joe nodded. "I know, but that was an accident. It's not as though he rammed our boat on purpose."

"I suppose not," Amy said. "Well, what are we going to do now?"

"Do?" Joe replied. "There's nothing we can do,

especially with the storm still raging outside."

Amy walked over to the porthole and gazed out. The storm was almost as fierce as before with the rain pelting the glass. But the thunder wasn't quite so loud and the lightning was less frequent.

Since there were two beds in the cabin, the girls chose one and the boys took the other. As the vessel tossed from side to side, it was very difficult to get to sleep but, eventually, they did.

~

As the sun crept above the horizon the following morning, Will yawned and climbed out of bed. As he peered through the porthole, he saw that the storm had ceased. The sea was looking calm again. In fact, it was eerily still. He then realised why. The boat wasn't moving at all. The motor had been turned off. Gazing upwards, he was able to see that there was not a single cloud in the sky. The storm had come quickly then gone equally quickly. Hearing a noise, he turned around and saw the girls getting out of bed.

"Did you sleep well?" Amy asked.

"Not really," Will admitted. "I seemed to be tossing and turning all night long, almost as much as the boat was."

Amy nodded. "I was the same."

A few minutes later, after the others had awoken, the children decided to head up on deck. The four of them made their way out of the cabin, down the hallway, and up the steps. As they entered the wheelhouse, they saw it was empty.

Joe frowned. "Where is everyone?"

"Maybe they're still sleeping," Will replied.

"Let's see if we can see any sign of land." Amy opened

the wheelhouse door and walked out onto the deck.

The four children scanned the horizon, hoping to see some sign of land but were dismayed to see nothing but water.

Joe sighed. What was going to happen to them?

## CHAPTER 3

# THE UNCHARTED ISLAND

Suddenly, just as they reached the stern of the boat, Will yelled out and pointed to the left of him. "Look! An island!"

The others crowded around and gazed out. The boy was right. A faint smudge of land could be seen in the distance. Was it an island? How big was it? Were people living there?

"I wonder if we'll head there," Amy said.

A second later, footsteps were heard and, turning around, the children saw Captain Red strolling towards them. "You're up early."

Will pointed to the smudge in the distance. "Is that the place you're heading for?"

"Maybe," Captain Red replied.

"What do you mean?" Amy questioned. "Don't you know where we are?"

Captain Red nodded. "In a manner of speaking. But the island I'm searching for isn't marked on any map."

Joe frowned. "What? How can that be? I thought all islands were marked on a map."

"Yes, all except the ones in the Bermuda Triangle, which is where we are," Captain Red replied. "The storm made it a bit difficult to navigate in a straight line but, if my estimates are correct, we are now roughly in the middle of the triangle."

"But isn't the triangle an area where countless boats have sunk?" Will asked.

Captain Red nodded. "Yes, it can be a very dangerous place. But what I'm searching for can only be found in the Bermuda Triangle so it's worth the risk."

"And what is that?" Sarah piped up.

"A white gorilla," Captain Red replied.

"You must be joking," Joe spluttered. "There's no such thing as a white gorilla."

"Wait, hold on, I do actually recall reading about something like that in an old newspaper," Will said. "There was a castaway who had spent several years drifting from one island to another. And, apparently, he saw a very tall white gorilla on one of the islands."

Captain Red nodded. "Yes, by his estimate the gorilla was over ten feet tall."

Amy frowned. "Just because some person who was lost at sea for several years told a reporter that he'd seen a large white gorilla doesn't mean that one exists. Besides, isn't the Bermuda Triangle a large place?"

"It is," Captain Red agreed. "So, we'll search the island in the distance and, if we don't find any unusual animals there, we'll continue to the next island."

~

By the time the boat came near to the island, they realised it was, in fact, two islands situated close together. One was very small and had a hill in the middle of it, while the other was quite large and mountainous. Since there was a cove in the larger one, Captain Red decided that would be the one they would explore first. Once the boat had dropped anchor, the men and the children climbed into the dinghy and rowed to the beach.

As they did so, Captain Red introduced his companions to the children. There was Spud, who was bald and had a potbelly, Lofty, whose face was almost completely hidden by a shaggy mane of hair and a wild beard. And, last of all, there was Slim and Bones, two men who looked almost identical, with thin faces and narrow noses.

Though Captain Red didn't say where the men were from, based on their dishevelled appearance, it was reasonable to suppose that they had escaped from the same prison as him.

Sarah thought the island looked like a tropical paradise since it had a border of white sand with palm trees dotted along the inner edge of it. She put her hand into the water. It was just the right temperature for swimming. However, this was certainly no time for swimming, so she followed the others up onto the beach.

Gazing around, Captain Red ordered his companions to start searching for any sign of life. However, after ten minutes scouring the beach and the nearby surroundings, it became evident that there was no one nearby.

Captain Red took out his pistol and fired a shot in the air just to see if anyone, or anything, would react. The only noise they heard was the chattering and squawking of some wild creatures off in the distance.

"Hmm, that sounded like birds and monkeys," Captain Red stated. "And, if there are monkeys living on this island, there should be some fruit trees. So, since we're low on food, I suggest we head inland to see if we can find some bananas or something else we can eat."

The group set off into the jungle and, before long, came upon a group of monkeys swinging through the trees. Joe hadn't been to the Caribbean very often, this was only the second time, but he was amazed to see that these monkeys had bright orange fur. He'd never seen any monkeys like this, and for that matter, neither had anyone else, not even Captain Red, who earlier had boasted to the children that he had sailed throughout the Caribbean.

The monkeys were fairly small, smaller than the average monkey and had very long tails. After searching for some time, no one could see any sign of banana trees or any other fruit tree, so they continued walking deeper into the jungle.

They had been walking for over an hour in the hot sun when they came to a clearing in the jungle. It was anyone's guess if humans had made the clearing or if the grass naturally grew here but, the good thing about it was that it was a change from the jungle. On the other side of the clearing, the land rose up steeply. They had reached the mountain that they had seen from the boat.

Sarah sighed and looked at Captain Red. "Can we please stop for a rest?"

Captain Red hesitated, thinking for a moment. "We haven't even explored half of the island yet."

"So what?" Joe questioned. "If you want to continue, maybe the four of us could rest somewhere while you explore."

Captain Red nodded. "Okay, you lot rest here. I want to see if there's a way over the mountain."

"How long are you going to be?" Will asked.

"I have no idea," Captain Red replied. "Just as long as it takes us to find some food." He turned to his companions. "Ready? Then, let's get going."

As the men resumed walking, Joe took a good look around and saw a narrow crevice in the side of the mountain. He turned to the others. "We could head over there and find a place to sit down."

"Okay," Will said.

The four of them walked over to the side of the mountain. Up close, they saw that it was a small cave, roughly seven feet deep. It was much cooler but there wasn't any place to lie down, so the children left the shelter of the cave and sought out a shady spot on the grass and waited for the men to return.

~

The men had been gone for just over an hour and the children were beginning to get a little concerned. Consequently, Will took it upon himself to see if he could see any sign of them. To do this, he needed to be higher up and so he looked around for a suitable tree to climb.

The others, especially the girls, weren't so keen on this idea, but Will was confident in his climbing abilities and so, after everyone wished him good luck, he started climbing. He made fast progress and had soon disappeared from view.

Sarah turned to Joe. "I hope he's going to be okay."

Joe nodded. "Well, he is a good climber, so..." The boy paused as he heard rustling in the nearby bushes.

It was so loud that all three turned towards the direction from which the noise was coming and got the shock of their lives as a huge creature emerged from the jungle.

## CHAPTER 4

# IT'S A MONSTER!

It was a white gorilla! Towering over ten feet tall, it looked like any other gorilla except for the fact that it was white and far larger than any they had ever seen. As soon as the animal caught sight of the children, he lumbered towards them.

"It's a monster!" Sarah exclaimed.

"What do we do?" Amy yelled.

"We need to run..." Joe paused as he quickly thought, and then an answer came to mind as he spotted the small cave. "In the cave, quick!"

The girls raced after Joe as he ran towards the cave which they had explored earlier. The animal loped after them, almost as though the children were the target in a game. Except, in this case, they didn't know what the gorilla would do to them if he caught them.

Luckily, the children reached the cave by the skin of their teeth and ran to the very back of it.

The gorilla roared out in anger and reached into the crevice with one of his hands. Fortunately, the cave became narrower as it went along and so the gorilla's hand could only reach halfway.

Amy breathed a sigh of relief. "We're safe."

"Yes, but what do we do now?" Sarah asked.

"Hope that the men return soon," Joe said. "Or that the animal gets bored and..." He frowned. "I think I hear Will."

"Oh no!" Amy shuddered. "Is he calling us?"

"I'm not sure," Joe replied. "I thought he would have heard the gorilla roar, so I'm not sure..."

The gorilla's hand suddenly withdrew from the cave.

Joe waited for a few seconds and slowly edged out to the entrance of the cave, the girls right behind him. They were just in time to see the gorilla start climbing the tree that Will had climbed up.

The three looked on in horror.

"Goodness!" Sarah exclaimed. "The gorilla is going after Will."

"How can we stop him?" Amy asked.

Joe shook his head. "We can't."

Unable to do anything, the children watched as the gorilla disappeared through the foliage as he climbed up the tree.

A few minutes later, there was a sound of breaking wood and a branch fell down. As it did so, the gorilla roared out.

Just at that moment, Captain Red and his men returned. As they walked along the grassy area, heading towards the children, they caught sight of the huge gorilla climbing down the tree.

They all stopped and stared. As the gorilla reached the ground and caught sight of them, the men started to back away in fright.

As the animal started to move towards the men, they fled into the jungle, heading for the cove.

Joe turned to the girls. "What are we going to do? Go with them or stay with Will?"

"We can't leave Will by himself," Amy said.

Sarah nodded. "I'm not leaving Will. Besides, Captain

Red and his men are running too fast for me."

"Yes, they are." Joe waited until the men and gorilla had disappeared from sight before he led the way over to the tall tree. Once there, he called up to Will. "Where are you?"

"I'm here!" Will yelled back a moment later.

Joe and the girls craned their necks in an attempt to see their friend and they were just able to do so. He was a long way up. "Are you coming down?"

"I can't!" Will shouted. "The gorilla broke one of the branches and now there's no way down."

"Oh no!" Sarah exclaimed, looking at the others. "No wonder the gorilla stopped climbing."

"Are you sure you can't get down?" Joe yelled.

"I'm positive," Will shouted.

Joe turned to the girls. "We'll have to get back to the cove and ask Captain Red for help."

"Oh, yes, maybe he'll have a rope," Sarah piped up.

Joe nodded and yelled out to Will. "We'll be back soon."

The three children hurried back to the cove. They were roughly halfway when they heard a noise up ahead and, a moment later, the gorilla emerged from the bushes.

"Hide!" Joe exclaimed.

Not wanting to be seen, the children left the path that Captain Red and his men had made and entered the thick jungle. After Joe was satisfied that they had travelled far enough away from the gorilla, he came to a halt.

The three of them stood still, listening. They waited until they could no longer hear the sound of the gorilla before deciding to walk back to the path.

However, this was easier said than done because the jungle was so dense that it was impossible to tell which way they had come from. Soon they were totally lost.

Joe sighed. "How did we manage to get lost?"

"I'm not sure," Amy replied. "Maybe if we head this way."

Joe and Sarah followed Amy for a minute or so until she suddenly yelled out. Joe stopped in shock as he saw Amy's feet disappear underneath her. He realised she had stepped into a bog. He reached out and dragged Sarah back to him. "Stop!"

"Help me!" Amy shouted, as she attempted to move her body. But she couldn't, she was just making the situation worse for herself.

Joe realised what was happening and called out to her. "Don't move! Stay as still as you can."

"Okay, but hurry!" Amy begged.

Joe turned to Sarah. "We need to find a long branch, or maybe even a long vine..." The boy paused as he caught sight of movement out of the corner of his eye. He peered around and saw a person with dark skin emerged from behind the bushes. He was dressed in the bare minimum and Joe realised the man was probably a native. He had no idea where he had come from, but that wasn't important right now. What was important was rescuing Amy. He called out. "Please help us!"

The native replied, but in a language not in English. The man then called out and, within a minute, several more dark skinned men appeared.

They all joined hands and pulled Amy out of the bog without any trouble.

Amy was so thankful that she had been rescued that, even though she didn't know if the men spoke English, she thanked them profusely.

Once she had finished speaking, the man grabbed her hand and dragged her away.

Joe frowned but, before he could do anything, the other men took hold of his and Sarah's arms. "Hey! What's going on!"

The men didn't reply. There was no use protesting since the men were stronger than them, so the children reluctantly went with the natives. They soon came across several canoes and, assuming that the natives wanted them to get into them, they did just that.

As the natives paddled the small canoes away from the island and towards the other island, the children gazed towards the cove to see if they could see the fishing vessel. But it was no longer there.

"Where has the boat gone?" Sarah asked.

"I don't know," Joe replied. "For all I know, these men could have done the same thing to Captain Red as they are doing to us."

"But why would the natives want to capture us?" Amy questioned.

"I don't know," Joe admitted. "However, I expect we'll find out soon."

# CHAPTER 5

# RUN!

After being led through a small village consisting mainly of reed huts, the children were pushed into one hut. A women joined them shortly afterwards and handed them what appeared to be bowls of soup.

As the children were hungry, they ate it. After the wooden bowls had been taken away, Joe turned to the girls. "I don't know what the natives want with us, but we need to escape." He walked to the front of the hut and looked out. As he saw a native sitting outside the neighbouring hut, he turned to the others. "If we escape out this way, we'll be spotted."

Sarah looked around the small hut. "But there's no other way out."

"Well, I should be able to make some kind of hole," Joe stated, peering around. A few moments later, he walked over to the back of the hut. "Since this hut is only made of reeds, it shouldn't take too long. However, since we have no idea what these natives will do to us if they find that we're trying to escape, someone needs to keep watch."

"I'll do that," Sarah volunteered.

"And I'll help you make the hole," Amy said.

The plan was put into motion and, for the next

five minutes, the only noise that was heard was the sound made by Joe and Amy as they attempted to break some of the reeds and make a hole in the back of the hut.

Luckily, no natives came to investigate, so there was no need for the two of them to pause and the soon had made a hole big enough to crawl through.

As soon as all three were out of the hut, Joe turned to the girls. "Let's make for that tall hill over there. If we climb to the very top, we'll be able to see how big this island is and it might help us decide what to do next."

"That sounds like a good idea," Amy said.

With the girls following, Joe led the way to the hill. As they got closer, Joe saw that it was in fact more like a mountain than a hill. But, since they had no other plans and nowhere else to go, they continued on.

However, as the terrain got steeper and the path that they had been following became no path at all, Amy paused for a moment. "Do you really think we should continue on?"

Joe peered down at the village below before he answered. "Do you think we should head back to the village and let the natives do whatever they were planning to do with us?"

"I didn't say that," Amy argued.

"Then what do you suggest?" Joe questioned. "If we don't go up this hill and see what else is on the island, what do you think we should do?"

"I don't know," Amy admitted.

"I'm getting sore legs," Sarah complained. "Can we rest for a while?"

"Well, how about you girls stay here and I'll continue on to the top?" Joe gazed upwards. "It isn't too far to go and there isn't any need for all of us to go."

"Okay, that sounds good." Sarah sat down on a rock. "You'll wait here with me won't you, Amy?"

Amy nodded. "Yes. Like Joe said, there's no need for all of us to go."

"I'll be back as soon as I can," Joe promised.

Joe continued walking, taking his time as the terrain became more difficult to traverse. He didn't want to go too fast and make a mistake. If something happened to him, it would just be the two girls, and he couldn't afford to make a mistake that might be costly. So, he made sure to take his time and not slip or stumble over the rocky ground.

The very top part of the mountain was devoid of trees and almost flat. From here, he could see the entire island. He saw that the village in which they had been imprisoned seemed to be the only village on the island. The jungle covered most of the island thus, while he couldn't be certain, it seemed as though that was the only part of the island where anyone was living.

Joe felt disappointed. He had hoped that there might be another part of the island where other people were living, some other place where they could go and get help. But there wasn't.

He sat down and closed his eyes. How he wished his parents were here with them. Surely, they would be able to convince the natives to help them and, even though the natives didn't speak English, he was sure his mother and father would still be able to do something. However, it was just the three of them, and it was the three of them that would have to rescue Will.

After sitting by himself for five minutes, he decided he should return to his sisters as they would probably be getting concerned. He stood up and glanced around one last time. He suddenly stiffened as he caught sight of a boat sailing around the far end of the island. He had no idea if it was Captain Red's boat, but he didn't care. Anyone was better than no one.

Joe hurried down the mountain, going as fast as he could. He almost slipped and a pile of rocks slid downwards. A few moments later, he heard the girls yell out in fright.

As they yelled out, he shouted back. A minute or two later, he was beside his sisters. He smiled at them. "I just saw a boat sailing along the other side of the island!"

"Is it the one belonging to Captain Red?" Sarah asked.

"I have no idea," Joe admitted. "However, I'm sure, whoever it is, will be able to help us. But we need to go as fast as possible."

The three children hurried down the slope, going as fast as their legs would take them. They feared they would be too late. As they arrived exhausted back at the place where the canoes were, they caught sight of the boat approaching. It was going to pass right by them.

Joe hurried over to the canoe that was nearest to the shore and the three of them pushed it into the water before they all clambered in. As there were only two paddles, Amy took one and Joe took the other while Sarah glanced backwards, wondering if the natives would notice them.

## CHAPTER 6

# A SCOUTING PARTY

Luckily, no one appeared as the three children paddled towards the boat. As they got closer, they saw it was, indeed, Captain Red's boat.

Joe continued paddling. "Even though Captain Red is probably an escaped prisoner, as so the rest of his crew are, I still think they're our best shot at rescuing Will."

As they got closer, the boat slowed down as though someone on board had seen them, and then, half a minute later, Captain Red appeared. "Where did you get the canoe from?"

"From the natives," Joe replied as he brought the canoe to a halt beside the vessel.

As Captain Red and Spud helped the three of them on board, he frowned. "Natives? Are you telling me there are natives on this island?"

Joe nodded. "Yes, but they don't speak English, which is why we need you."

Captain Red frowned. "Me? You need me? Why? Hey, where's the other kid? There were four of you before."

Amy nodded. "Yes, that's right. Will's trapped up a tree and we need your help to rescue him."

“How did he get trapped up a tree?” Captain Red asked.

The children quickly explained what had happened to them since he and his men had left them. As they talked, he stroked his red beard. Once they had finished speaking, he nodded. “I was planning on going back to that island anyway to capture some animals, but it’s getting quite late and—”

“We need to rescue Will tonight!” Amy interrupted.

Captain Red shook his head. “That is impossible. It would be dark before we even reached the tree and so it would be foolhardy to set off now. But, we can have an early start in the morning because, just before you came on board, I laid out a plan with my men to capture the gorilla tomorrow. So, we can find your friend first and then put my plan into motion.”

The following morning, an hour after they had set off, the group reached the tree that Will had climbed.

Joe called out. “Will! We’re back!”

There was no reply.

A few moments later, all three children called out at the top of their voices. Again, no reply was heard.

“I wonder where he is,” Sarah said anxiously, a look of concern on her face.

“Well, he certainly isn’t up the tree,” Captain Red said.

“Maybe he managed to climb down last night,” Bones said.

“I doubt it,” Joe said.

“Well, I’ve climbed my fair share of trees in the past,” Lofty stated. “Let me have a crack at it.”

The group watched on as the tall man walked over

to the trunk and started climbing up. Within a few moments, he had scrambled up and was making steady progress until he came to the spot where the branch had broken off.

He clung there for a short while as he sought some way to get up the tree, but he couldn't. He finally shook his head and climbed back down.

"So, that means that Will couldn't have climbed down," Sarah piped up.

Captain Red nodded. "If a tall man like Lofty couldn't climb up, then no child could have climbed down."

"So where is he?" Amy asked, bewildered.

"I think I may have answer." Slim pointed to a ledge halfway up the side of the mountain. "Maybe the kid jumped onto that."

Lofty nodded. "That's what I think too. I couldn't see much from up the tree, but I did spot that ledge and, while I couldn't be certain, there seemed to be a cave of some sort next to it."

"But, if Will was sitting in the cave, why wouldn't he hear us?" Amy questioned.

"Well, maybe it's not just a cave, maybe it's a tunnel," Captain Red suggested. "It might even lead to the other side of the mountain. Anyways, it's clear that the boy is not here. So let's proceed with catching the gorilla."

"But what about Will?" Sarah wailed. "If he's on the other side of the mountain—"

"Look! I've done what I said I would do," Captain Red roared. "Once I catch the gorilla, if the boy is still missing, I'll have another look for him. But now it's time to move on."

Reluctantly, the children followed Captain Red away from the tree and towards the shore. They had been walking for ten minutes or so when the man paused and walked over to a banana tree. He smiled. "Some animal has been eating these bananas recently."

"It might have been a monkey," Spud commented.

Captain Red nodded. "Maybe. But it also could have been a gorilla. Either way, we'll dig a trap here."

While the children sat down by the base of the tree, the men got to work digging a hole. They then cut down branches and palm fronds and laid them over the hole so that it was hidden.

It took over three hours for a big enough hole to be dug and hidden and, while everyone had a rest, Captain Red examined the work that had just been done. "This should be satisfactory. Now we just need to put some bananas in the middle."

Being careful not to fall in, the men placed several in the middle of the trap. Once that was done, Captain Red turned to the others. "Now we wait. Take up your positions and make sure you don't make a sound. And stay well hidden. We don't want the gorilla seeing us before he reaches the trap."

The men split up. Captain Red motioned to the children. "You come with me."

The children obeyed without question and, after Captain Red found a secluded spot under a large bush, they sat down and waited. None of the children were very comfortable but, since they knew it would be pointless to complain, they didn't.

Time passed slowly. Very slowly indeed. Since the group had set off very early in the morning, it was only just past noon. The children were glad that they weren't in view of the sun as it was quite hot even in the shade.

Several times, the children complained to Captain Red, but he took no notice. He was determined to catch the gorilla and wasn't going to let anyone, especially children, get in his way. Since the children wanted his help to find Will, they hoped the gorilla would appear soon.

They were in luck. As the sun reached its peak in the sky, the children heard a noise out of the ordinary. Something, or someone, was moving towards them. And, from the noise it was making, it was a big creature.

Joe's heart was in his mouth as he caught sight of the gorilla loping through the bushes.

Captain Red smiled, but didn't say anything.

The gorilla slowly approached the trap. As he spotted the fruit, he slightly changed direction so that he was heading directly for the hole.

Time seemed to tick by awfully slowly as the creature got closer and closer to the hole. Then, just like that, the animal's legs disappeared from sight as the gorilla reached the hole. A second later, he tumbled down, giving an anguished cry as he did so.

Captain Red stood up and yelled out. "Attack!"

All of the men suddenly emerged from their hiding spots and ran towards the hole. As the gorilla flung his arms about and attempted to clamber out of the hole, the men reached into their rucksacks and started throwing bottles of chloroform at him.

The animal bellowed out in anger and stretched his arms out in an attempt to get the men. But the men retreated until they were just out of his reach. The gorilla thudded his arms against his chest and then, with an almighty heave, started crawling out of the hole.

Amy's face took on a look of shock as she realised that the gorilla was now free. Not only that, but the animal was angry. Very angry indeed.

## CHAPTER 7

# CHLOROFORM

Captain Red reached into his rucksack and picked up two bottles of chloroform.

As the gorilla slowly rose to his feet, Captain Red darted forward. He ducked and jumped to avoid the animal as he lunged out with his arms.

Then, standing right beside the creature, Captain Red flung the bottles of chloroform directly at the animal's face.

This, along with all the other bottles that the men were throwing, was the final straw. The gorilla wobbled for a few seconds and, as he did so, Captain Red rushed back to the children.

A few moments later, the gorilla's legs collapsed and he fell back into the hole.

Everyone, except the children, roared in delight. As the men rushed forward to make sure that the creature was, in fact, unconscious, Sarah turned to her brother and sister. "I was almost hoping that the gorilla would escape."

Amy nodded. "Me too. But I was conflicted between two thoughts, rescuing Will and the gorilla going free. Because, as much as I like all animals, I really want to rescue Will. So, hopefully Captain Red will fulfil his end of the bargain and help us search for Will now."

The children walked over to the trap and had a good look at the creature. Up close, the gorilla looked like any other gorilla. Just bigger than average and white. Joe had no idea why various creatures on this island were bigger than average, but he felt sorry that it was the animal's size that had led to his downfall. If he had been smaller, the men wouldn't have been interested in him at all.

Suddenly, Lofty yelled out. "I don't believe it."

Everyone looked in the direction in which Lofty had pointed. A baby gorilla had emerged from behind a tree. It was weeping.

Straight away, the children realised that the gorilla in the trap was the mother. As the baby caught sight of his mother trapped in the hole, he ran as fast as his little legs could take him.

As the animal did so, Captain Red yelled out. "Capture the baby!"

The young gorilla didn't stand a chance against the onslaught. After all, he was just a baby and nowhere near the size of his mother. After struggling for a bit, and attempting to bite Spud, the creature was lassoed in such a way that he could no longer move.

"Shall we throw another bottle on the baby?" Spud asked.

Captain Red shook his head. "No, save it. This baby isn't going to cause trouble. Besides, sooner or later, his mother will wake up. When she does, we'll need as much chloroform as we can get. In the meantime, we can take the baby back to boat and plan what to do next. If we can't get the mother on board, we'll just take the baby back to the mainland and, using the money that we'll get from selling the animal, we'll buy a larger boat and get more men. Then, we can come back and not only capture the gorilla, but other creatures."

"What about the police?" Lofty asked. "Won't they still be looking for us?"

Captain Red shook his head. "I'm sure they've got bigger problems to deal with. Besides, with all the money we're going to get, we can buy a faster vessel, one that will outrun the patrol boats. However, for the time being, let's get back to the boat with the baby." He turned to Slim and Bones, the two men who were closest to him. "You stay here and guard the gorilla. I'll send the back with more chloroform as soon as I can."

"But what happens if the animal wakes up in the meantime?" Bones questioned.

"She's not going to, not with the amount of chloroform we flung at her. However, in case she does, take this." Captain Red reached into his pocket and pulled out a flare gun. "If you fire it, we'll come straight away."

Slim took the flare gun. "Okay, but you had better be quick. I don't want to be left in this jungle when the sun goes down."

"Me neither." Captain Red turned to the other men. "Give all the chloroform you have left to the two men who are staying behind. Then we'll get going."

"But what about Will?" Joe asked. "When are you going to search for him?"

"Not until we get the baby gorilla on board the boat," Captain Red replied. "However, feel free to call out to your friend as we walk back just in case he is within hearing distance."

Joe nodded. "We'll do that."

Once the baby gorilla had been tied down on a makeshift plank, the group departed. While the men took turns carrying the animal, the children strode out in front, shouting out to Will.

All three knew that there was only a very slim

chance he would reply but, as long as there was still a chance, they were determined to try.

By the time they arrived back at the beach, the children were hoarse from yelling out. Their yells hadn't yielded any response, but at least they had tried.

The trickiest task now was to get the gorilla into the dinghy.

Luckily, since the baby had been resisting for the whole trip, he was now quite exhausted and they were able to get the animal on board without too much difficulty.

Once the gorilla had been locked in a cage, Captain Red called out to his men. "Let's have a drink to celebrate."

"But what about the chloroform?" Lofty asked.

"Relax, Slim and Bones can wait," Captain Red replied.

A few minutes later, the children could hear the tinkling of glasses and the jolly laughter of the men. Wanting to get away from the noise, the children walked to the stern of the boat and looked out towards the beach.

"I wonder where Will is right now," Amy said.

Joe sighed and put his arms around both of his sisters. "I'm sure he's somewhere safe. If anyone can survive out there in the jungle, it's Will. He's a pretty resourceful boy."

Sarah nodded. "Yes, Will is an amazing boy. He can climb almost anything and he's smart as well."

"And he's gone camping a lot," Amy pointed out. "And this is just like camping without any supplies."

The children paused talking for a few moments while they imagined what Will might be doing this very second.

Suddenly, there was a noise near the beach.

Amy frowned. "I wonder what..." She drew in a sharp breath as she and the others caught sight of a white gorilla as it emerged from behind the trees and lumbered onto the beach.

# CHAPTER 8

# STUCK

As the animal reached the sandy shore, she pounded her arms against her chest and roared out in anger.

"It's the gorilla!" Sarah yelled.

Joe frowned. "That's impossible! What about the two men guarding her?"

"No idea, but we need to tell Captain Red," Amy exclaimed as the gorilla waded into the water. "The animal is coming directly towards us."

Joe nodded. "This isn't good."

All three raced back to the cabin and Joe flung open the door. The men were in the middle of singing a rowdy song.

Desperate to get their attention, Joe screamed out. "The gorilla is coming!"

The singing stopped and Captain Red frowned at the boy. "What did you say?"

"The gorilla is coming for us!" Joe shouted.

"He's in the water right now!" Amy yelled.

"But that's impossible," Captain Red spluttered. "There's no way—"

"See for yourself!" Sarah piped up.

Captain Red put down his glass and followed the children out of the cabin. The other men followed behind them.

The smile on Captain Red's face disappeared as he caught sight of the gorilla wading towards them. "It's true."

"I didn't think gorillas or monkeys liked water," Spud muttered.

"No, they don't." Captain Red took out his pistol and aimed it at the creature. "But this might be the exception. Shoot at it, but don't aim to kill it." A second later, he fired his weapon.

The girls, and even Joe, put their hands over their ears as the shots rang out. As the bullets whistled past the gorilla, the beast paused and turned around.

As the animal retreated back to the beach, Captain Red laughed. "Well, it didn't take much to scare her." He paused. "I wonder what happened to Slim and Bones." He turned to the children. "You didn't see any sign of a flare, did you?"

Joe shook his head. "No."

Captain Red slowly nodded. "Okay, well, let's start by organising a group to go and find them."

"I'm not going out into the jungle," Lofty stated. "Not while that gorilla is loose."

"But you saw how scared she was of a few bullets," Captain Red argued. "So, if you come in sight of her, just do what we just did here."

"And what will you be doing?" Spud questioned.

"Working out our next plan of action," Captain Red replied.

Captain Red thought for a moment. "Well, if no one wants to go, I suppose we could sail out of this cove and moor somewhere closer to Slim and Bones. That way, we'll be away from where the gorilla currently is."

"Yes, let's do that," Spud agreed.

Everyone got to work and it wasn't long before the

boat engine roared to life. Soon, the craft was steadily moving towards the entrance of the cove.

The children stayed by the railing, keeping their eyes glued to the beach, wondering if the gorilla was going to appear. But there was no sign of the animal.

"I wonder why the men didn't fire the flare gun," Joe muttered.

"Maybe they got scared and ran away as soon as the gorilla woke up," Sarah suggested.

"Possibly," Joe said. "I suppose we'll find out the truth soon. But it's going to be awfully difficult to find the two men unless they stick close to the trap."

Suddenly, the boat shuddered to a stop.

Amy frowned. "Why have we stopped?"

"I've no idea," Joe admitted. "The engine is still running, but we're not moving."

A few moments later, the motor stopped just as Lofty, with a knife in his hand, emerged from the cabin. He made his way to the rear of the boat and climbed over the railing. Then, putting the handle of the knife between his teeth, he used both hands to climb down into the water.

"The boat must be stuck on something," Sarah said.

Joe nodded. "Yes, that's what it looks like."

The children hurried over to the place where Lofty had climbed over and glanced down just as he disappeared underneath the water.

As they watched, Spud walked over to them. "Did Lofty just go into the water?"

Joe nodded. "Yes, he did. But I'm not sure what he's doing."

"Well, Lofty is…" Spud paused as the tall man swam up to the surface.

As Lofty caught sight of Spud, he called out. "Tell Captain Red that it's going to take some time to free the propellers. The reeds have jammed around the metal."

Spud nodded. "Will do."

All was silent for a minute or so as the man went to speak to Captain Red and Lofty bobbed underneath the water again.

Joe glanced at the girls. "At least this didn't happen when the gorilla was wading towards us."

Sarah nodded. "Yes, that wouldn't have been good."

"Hey!" Amy shouted. "Look!"

Joe and Sarah looked in the direction in which Amy had pointed. Only bushes and rocks could be seen at first and then Joe's heart leaped into his throat as he saw the angry face of the gorilla staring at them. "Oh no!"

Sarah also saw the gorilla as she emerged from the bushes and stepped onto the rocks. "The animal is back!"

As the creature climbed down off the rocks and waded into the water, Joe quickly spun around. He realised with dismay that the vessel had come to a stop in the worst possible place. They were at the entrance to the cove and, as such, were at the closest point to land since the entrance was narrow. And, since reeds had become entwined around the propeller, Joe assumed there was probably a reef underneath them, thus making the water shallower than any other part of the cove.

These two things meant one thing. The gorilla was in the perfect position to reach them. She couldn't have done so earlier, but now the situation was different.

## CHAPTER 9

# THE BATTLE

Suddenly, Spud yelled out. "The gorilla is back!"

It wasn't long before Captain Red appeared on deck. He took one look at the creature and then disappeared down the steps. He was back shortly carrying chloroform.

As the seconds ticked by, the gorilla got closer and closer to the trapped vessel. Lofty quickly appeared and climbed up over the railing again. He ran over to Captain Red. "The propeller is fixed."

"Good to hear." Captain Red glanced over at Spud. "Throw everything we have at the beast."

The men did just that. However, this time, the bottles didn't do any good. Maybe because the men were throwing them in fear and thus their aim wasn't as precise as it should have been, or maybe it was because the animal was trying to avoid the bottles.

Either way, it soon became clear to Captain Red that a change of tactics was needed. He ran into the cabin and started the engines.

As soon as the propellers began to spin and the vessel began moving once more, the gorilla roared out. She quickly increased her speed and reached out, grabbing a rope that was tied around the front of the vessel. As Spud threw the last bottle of chloroform, they watched the tug of war unfold between the boat and the creature.

The gorilla was more powerful than the boat and was soon dragging the boat backwards towards the shallow part of the reef. Suddenly, everyone heard the agonising groan of the vessel as the animal dragged it over the reef. Once the gorilla was satisfied that the boat was stuck, she let go.

Even though the engine was still running, the vessel didn't move an inch. It was powerless.

With one big lunge, the animal reached out with her arm and grabbed Lofty around the waist. She pulled him away from the boat and flung her arm back. A moment later, the man went sailing up into the air, landing in the water far away.

As soon as Spud saw this, fear took over. He stopped what he was doing and ran to the other end of the boat. Upon reaching the stern, he dived into the water and swam away, increasing the distance between him and the gorilla.

"We should do the same!" Amy yelled.

Joe hesitated. As much as he wanted to run away, he just couldn't shake the feeling that no animal would be this angry unless there was a specific reason. He knew the men had tried to trap the animal earlier, but he still thought there was a bigger reason.

As the creature started tearing the boat apart, Joe realised something. "Of course! No wonder the gorilla is so mad."

"Whatever are you talking about?" Sarah questioned.

"She's looking for her baby!" Joe replied. "If we give the baby back to her, she might leave us in peace."

"Who knows what the gorilla is going to do," Amy muttered. "Let's play it safe and hide."

"No, I need your help," Joe said. "And Sarah's."

Amy turned to Sarah. "What do you think we should do?"

Sarah's reply was instant. "Get the baby!"

With a slight smile, Joe nodded. "Okay, let's get to the storeroom."

The children raced down the steps and all the way down the hallway to the storeroom. Inside were a number of empty cages and, at the far end, in one of the largest cages, lay the baby.

As the children rushed over, Joe wondered why the animal wasn't moving. Surely he or she had heard the mother. But, for some reason, the animal was asleep.

"Maybe one of the men gave the baby a dose of the chloroform," Amy suggested.

Joe nodded. "Yes, probably. But how are we going to get the gorilla up to the deck?"

Sarah peered through the cage. "How are we even going to get the animal out of the cage?"

Amy tugged on the padlock. "We need to find the key."

The three children paused as they heard the frightened scream of a man and the roar of the gorilla.

"Whatever we are going to do, we need to do it quickly," Joe said.

"I just don't see how..." Amy paused as she heard footsteps. "One of the men is coming."

"What are we going to do?" Sarah asked.

Joe tried to think of a plan but, before he could come up with one, Captain Red's face appeared. "Why are you still here? You need to get off the boat! The gorilla has gone crazy—"

"She just wants her baby!" Joe shouted.

"Baby?" Captain Red frowned. "Of course, why didn't I think of that. Maybe that will calm the animal down."

"Do you have the keys to the cage?" Amy asked.

Captain Red nodded as he fumbled in his pocket. "I don't know how we can carry the baby…" He paused as daylight suddenly flooded the darkened room as some of the wood near the window was ripped away.

A few seconds later, they saw the angry face of the gorilla staring directly at them.

Shocked, and scared, Captain Red attempted to find the key to unlock the cage.

As soon as the gorilla caught sight of her child, she bellowed out in anger and tore more of the wood away to create a bigger hole.

"Quick!" Joe yelled.

"I'm hurrying as fast as I can!" Captain Red shouted.

As the gorilla reached into the storeroom with one of her arms, the children shrunk back, not wanting to get in the way of the angry creature.

# CHAPTER 10

# SMASHED APART

Fortunately, just at that moment, Captain Red found the right key and flung open the door of the cage. He stood back and watched as the gorilla grabbed hold of the cage and pulled it closer to the hole.

The animal then turned it around so that the open door of the cage was facing her. She reached in and lovingly took hold of the baby. She put the youngster onto her shoulders with one arm.

With the other arm, she took hold of the cage and smashed it down onto the floor of the storeroom. She did this once, then twice, then three times.

By now, Captain Red had managed to convince the children to head for the stairs and it was fortunate that they did just that for, on the third attempt at smashing the cage, water started flooding into the room.

The children hurried down the hallway and up the stairs as water quickly rose. As they reached the deck, they glanced around. They were shocked to see that all that remained of the wheelhouse was broken timber and shattered glass.

Captain Red took one sorrowful look at the controls and shook his head. "There's no way this vessel will be moving ever again."

"Well, at least the gorilla is happy now," Amy stated.

"What? Why do..." Sarah paused as she looked in the direction in which Amy was gazing and saw the gorilla, along with her baby, heading towards the island. She smiled and hugged her sister. "I was so scared earlier. I wasn't sure what was going to happen to us."

Amy smiled as she looked into the green eyes of her sister. "I would never allow anything to happen to you."

"Me neither," Joe announced, wrapping his arms around both of them.

"Enough with the hugging, we've got work to do," Captain Red stated.

"Work?" Joe questioned. "What work?"

"We've got to transport as much stuff as we can to the land," Captain Red replied. "I doubt the gorilla will return but, even if she doesn't, it's clear we can't spend the night here."

"Can't your friends do that?" Amy asked. "We're just children."

"They can but, if you don't want to sleep on the grass and go without food, then you'll pitch in and help." Captain Red peered up at the sky. "It's going to get dark soon and we don't have time to waste. Once we've transported everything, I'm going to see what Slim and Bones have to say for themselves."

~

As the group arrived at the place where the gorilla had been caught earlier, the children stared in shock. The gorilla was still in the hole fast asleep.

In shock, Joe turned to the girls. "There must be two giant gorillas."

Amy slowly nodded. "Yes."

Captain Red was astounded. "What a stroke of luck! Imagine how much money we're going to make with two huge gorillas."

"Well, if there are two, there are likely to be more than two," Spud pointed out.

"Yes, maybe even a whole family." Captain Red turned to the two men he had left behind and quickly explained the situation to them.

"So, what are we going to do about this gorilla? It's probably going to wake up soon and when it does…" Slim suddenly paused as the gorilla started to move.

Slim and Bones tossed two bottles of chloroform at the creature in an attempt to subdue it. As they did so, one of the men called out. "The other gorilla is coming!"

Everyone turned around and saw the other gorilla with her baby clutched around her neck. The animal loped towards them.

Captain Red quickly made a decision as he gazed at the bottles of chloroform. He turned to his companions. "We should retreat as fast as we can and come back another day."

As the men ran away, the children followed them as fast as their feet could carry them.

Luckily, the other gorilla no longer seemed interested in the humans and made her way to her companion in the hole. As they ran away, the gorilla roared out and banged her chest as if to warn them not to attempt to meddle with her again.

The children ignored the animal's outburst but, as they continued to run, they began to notice some of the monkeys gazing at them. It didn't take long for Joe to realise that the big gorilla had been trying to send a message to the other animals.

After a while, the group slowed down and began to walk instead of run, confident that they were out of harms way.

Suddenly, Captain Red, who was at the front of the group, came to a stop as he saw a number of monkeys hovering at the base of a large tree.

While these monkeys were a lot smaller than the gorillas, they are still bigger than the average monkey. They are chattering to one another and leaping up and down on ground.

Captain Red paused, wondering what was going on. As the group waited for him to give an order, one of the monkeys picked up a round piece of yellow fruit that had fallen off the tree and threw it at them.

As the fruit whistled by Captain Red, he took out his pistol and fired one shot at the monkey who had thrown the fruit. As the bullet slammed into the tree, the monkeys scattered, quickly disappearing from sight.

Captain Red smiled. "That scared them off."

Lofty glanced behind him. "Let's get going before the gorilla decides to come after us."

Captain Red resumed walking and headed in the direction of the monkeys. He had barely gone two feet before something hard slammed into his left leg. "Aggh!" He hopped about in agony as the round, brown object rolled around on the ground. It was a coconut.

Angry, and determined to get rid of the monkey's once and for all, Captain Red fired his pistol into the undergrowth. He kept on firing until he was out of bullets. As silence fell, everyone in the group looked around, wondering if the monkey's had been scared off.

A second later, the answer was revealed when a

piece of fruit flew towards them. Then another lot of fruit.

Within a minute, everyone was ducking to avoid being hit by the hard, and sometimes soft objects, depending on how ripe the fruit was.

## CHAPTER 11

# SLITHERING REPTILES

"Retreat!" Captain Red yelled.

"But our camp is in the other direction!" Spud shouted.

"Go that way if you want, but I'm not going to get injured by a bunch of animals," Captain Red argued. "We'll take the long way around."

Joe turned to the girls. "I'm not game to go through the monkeys, what about you?"

Amy shook her head. "No, let's follow Captain Red."

It wasn't long before everyone was following Captain Red. As the children heard the yelps of the animals, they glanced back and couldn't believe their eyes.

The monkeys, some clutching fruit in their mouths, had left the safety of the trees and were running after them. Other monkeys were high up in the tree branches leaping from one tree to another.

"Come on!" Joe yelled.

The animals had quite a good aim and, while everyone hoped to not get a bruise or two, none of them wanted to be stuck in the jungle all alone and at the mercy of the monkeys. Especially since no one knew what other animals they might have to face.

It was quite a chaotic five or so minutes as the men

yelled to one another, dodging fruit and bushes as they did so.

Every now and then, one of the men fired his pistol at the monkeys, but this didn't seem to have any major effect.

Joe raced alongside the girls, wanting to protect them as best he could. Sarah was the most vulnerable since she couldn't run as fast.

However, in this case, he couldn't help but admire the effort she was putting in, almost matching him and Amy's footsteps stride by stride.

A minute later, Joe frowned. Something was amiss. It took a moment or two, and then he realised that it was a lot quieter than before. The monkeys must have stopped chasing them. He paused for a moment to make sure that this was the case and saw that he was, in fact, correct.

Joe wondered why, but soon the answer was at hand. As he ran after the girls, the jungle parted to give way to reeds as far as the eye could see.

It immediately became clear to Joe that the monkeys were afraid of whatever lived in the swamp. However, not wanting to be left behind by the men, the children kept on running.

They were almost at the group when Lofty yelled out. "Look out!"

The children ran up beside the men and glanced through the reeds as a big, blue reptile opened his mouth and slid his tongue out, waving it back and forth. As he did so, the animal began to waddle towards them. It was far bigger and longer than any lizard that the children had seen.

However, as the lizard was slower than the monkeys, it didn't take too much effort to run away from him. But, a few seconds later, another big lizard emerged from the reeds and blocked the way the group had just come.

Searching for a way out, the men and children headed in another direction. The soft ground soon turned to water but, since no one wanted to turn back and face the two lizards that were still waddling after them, the group continued on.

Luckily, the water wasn't even ankle deep and so, while the children's shoes got wet, that was all. Suddenly, Slim fell over.

A moment later, Bones yelled out in horror. "Snake!"

Captain Red took out a small hunting knife and attempted to stop the snake as the tail of the animal wrapped himself around the legs of Slim.

Scared of the snake, the children stayed back, so much so that they were the only ones to catch sight of movement to the right of them. It only lasted for a brief second but, through the small gap in the reeds, Joe thought he had caught sight of a canoe.

Positive it was the natives, he ran away from the group, stumbled over the boggy ground, and parted the reeds so he could have a better view of what lay ahead.

He grimly smiled. He had been correct. To the right of him, a number of natives, in three wooden canoes, were paddling away. Joe put his hands up and beckoned to them as he yelled out. "Please help us!"

It wasn't long before the canoes had turned around and the men were paddling towards Joe, who had now been joined by his sisters.

Amy got the shock of her life when she saw a familiar face. "It's Uti!"

Sarah was overjoyed. "Hooray! We can go home!"

As the canoe came to a stop, Uti climbed out and hugged them. "I can't believe I found you. It's so good to see you all. Hey, where's Will?"

Joe sighed. "He's disappeared."

As Uti caught sight of movement in the swamp, he frowned. "Who are those men?"

"Escaped prisoners," Joe replied. "They rescued us when our boat sank and now one of them is being attacked by a snake."

Uti nodded and motioned to the natives to follow him. The men did so without question, two of them holding long, curved steel knives.

As the group reached Captain Red and his men, they saw that the situation had turned worse. Now there were two snakes slithering about.

While Lofty and Spud were too scared to do anything, Bones was trying to untangle the slippery reptiles from Slim's legs. But the snakes clearly had no intention of letting go. Captain Red was still thrashing about with his hunting knife, but he wasn't making any progress.

Suddenly, one of the snakes lunged out at Captain Red and bit him on the side of his face. Captain Red's knife dropped from his hands and he fell to his knees in pain.

A moment later, the natives attacked the snakes with their long knives. The injured snakes immediately released their grip on the humans and slithered away into the reeds.

One of the natives hurried over to the fallen man and examined him. He then looked at Uti and, in stilted English, indicated that the man needed to go with them or else he would die.

Suddenly, Slim yelled out and everyone looked to where he was pointing. They spotted two monster lizards scuttling towards them.

As the natives brandished their knives, Uti turned

to the men. "Do you have a boat nearby?"

Bones shook his head. "No."

Uti nodded. "Come with us then. We should have enough room if we all squeeze in."

## CHAPTER 12

# SOS

As the natives paddled the canoes towards the other island, Uti turned to the children. "It's good to see you're safe. I really was worried about you. Now, tell me about Will."

Joe and the girls quickly told their friend all they knew about Will's disappearance.

As they reached the island, all thoughts turned to Captain Red who was now unconscious. As the natives lifted him up, the group followed them to one of the huts. Several drops of a reddish coloured liquid were dropped into his mouth and the natives indicated that he would soon be well again.

Uti and children stepped outside. The man looked at his watch. "Since we only have a few hours until sunset, I'll have to make every minute count if I'm going to find Will."

"We're coming with you," Joe stated.

Uti frowned. "I'm not sure that's a good idea. I was—"

"We need as many eyes searching for Will as we can get," Joe interrupted.

"And I'm not staying here with the natives after what happened last time," Sarah piped up.

Uti shook his head. "From what I can gather, these natives seem like good people."

"Then why did they treat us as though we were their prisoners?" Amy questioned.

"For your own safety no doubt. You're just children." Uti sighed. "Okay, you can come with me, but only if you do as I say at all times. Now, since we don't know where Will is, we'll have to fly low over the entire island."

Leaving the natives to take care of the escaped prisoners, Uti and the children hurried over to where a small red and blue aircraft was parked. They all climbed into the plane and, a few moments later, with a whir of engines, the aircraft started taxiing across the grass.

It wasn't long before it left the ground, soaring steeply up into the air. But it didn't last long since Uti quickly levelled out. He had no intention of going higher than just above the treetops. It was essential that they had the best chance possible to see any sign of Will and they couldn't do that if the plane was too high.

Within five minutes, the plane was over the other island and, from then on, everyone's eyes were glued to the trees below as they stared through the windows looking for any sign of Will. Uti zigzagged back and forth along the island until they had covered every part except the valley. Since the mountain was very steep, Uti had to open up the throttle and take some time for the plane to gain altitude.

As soon as he was above the mountain, Uti levelled out the plane and dipped down the nose. He decreased the engine power until the plane was almost stalling, thus giving them the best chance to see anything that would indicate that Will was in the valley.

Straight away, the children noticed something

distinctive about the valley. There was a big, deep lake in the middle and, surrounding it, a number of very tall trees, much taller than any tree they had ever seen. Apart from this, the entire valley was covered in bright green grass. There were also some strange looking red and yellow bushes.

There was still no sign of Will. Or, for that matter, anyone. But they did see lots of gorillas. Their white fur stood out against the lush green. They were mainly around the lake. Some of them were in the trees, some of them were lying on the grass, and some of them were even having a dip in the water.

As the plane glided across the valley, Joe's heart began to sink. It was beginning to look as though they had been wrong. Will wasn't there.

Suddenly, Joe saw it. He yelled out, pointing downwards as he did so. "Look! Will must have done that!"

Everyone looked down and saw that someone had made an SOS sign out of tree branches.

Amy clapped her hands in joy. "That must have been put there by Will!"

"How are we going to get there?" Sarah asked. "I can't see any place to land."

Uti veered the plane upwards. "I can't see a clear strip of land that's long enough to land the plane on either."

"What are you doing?" Joe questioned. "Why are you flying away—"

"If we're going to explore the valley, we're going to need more people," Uti interrupted. "And, since Captain Red and his men have weapons, they will be the ideal group of people to work with since I'm sure there will be some dangerous animals in that valley."

Joe sighed as Uti turned the plane back towards the other island. "But will they want to help us?"

Uti nodded. "I believe so. After all, I did help save Captain Red's life. If I hadn't come along when I did, he probably would have been dead by now. So, hopefully, he will repay the favour."

~

Twenty minutes later, now with Captain Red and his men aboard, the red and blue aircraft approached the grassy area near the ledge.

Everyone held their breath as the plane got lower and lower. Sarah thought the patch of grass seemed very narrow and not very long. Could it really be long enough for the plane? She, along with the others, were about to find out.

Thankfully, it was. As the wheels came to a stop a few moments later, she breathed a sigh of relief. "That was too close."

"Yes, it was a bit close," Uti admitted.

"Come on, let's get going." Joe climbed out of his seat and walked over to the door.

"Wait! You're not going!" Uti exclaimed.

"What? Of course I am," Joe stated.

Uti shook his head. "No, it could be too dangerous in the valley. I will be staying with you and your sisters while Captain Red and his men go and find Will."

"But isn't it best if we all go and find Will?" Sarah asked. "You know, the more people the better?"

Captain Red shook his head. "Not in this case, young lady. You lot will only slow me down."

Joe sighed. "Okay." He really would have liked to have gone with the men but, as the group packed ropes, torches, and guns into the rucksacks and moved off, Joe realised this was not a mission for children and it was better if they stayed behind.

# CHAPTER 13

# AN UNEXPECTED PASSENGER

As they reached the spot below the ledge, Amy gazed upwards. It seemed so steep that she wondered if it was actually going to be possible for the men to climb up there.

However, Lofty had a different plan in mind. He walked over to the tree and quickly climbed up. Once he reached the spot with the broken branch, he took out a coiled up rope and threw that over one of the higher branches. As the other end came back down, he started climbing up the rope.

Once he no longer had any need of the rope, he coiled it up and continued climbing. Before long, he had jumped across to the ledge. He disappeared from sight for a minute and then reappeared, tossing the rope down as he did so. "I found a tunnel!"

Uti smiled. "Good, that clears up one mystery then." He turned to Captain Red. "See if you can see any sign of Will after you leave the tunnel."

Captain Red nodded. "I'll do that. I'll be back before dark."

"Good idea," Uti replied. "I don't think it would be good for you to be wandering around the valley in the darkness. Besides, if you haven't found Will in the next hour or so, I don't think you'll find him when it gets dark."

Uti and the children watched on as the men, using the rope for support, climbed up the steep slope. Once everyone had reached the top and had disappeared from view, Uti turned to the children. "I think it's best if we head back to the plane for the time being since the men will be at least an hour."

Joe nodded. "Yes, there's no use standing here all that time."

The group walked back to the plane in silence. They had just reached the aircraft when, suddenly, a gunshot rang out, then another, and then another. Within the next ten seconds or so, more gunshots, too many to count, rang out in quick succession.

Uti, just like the children, was stunned. "What is going on?"

"Let's go back and see!" Amy exclaimed.

As they ran back, silence reigned once more. By the time they arrived below the ledge, there was still no further sound of any gunshots and, as they gazed up, there was no sign of anyone.

"I wonder what just happened," Joe muttered.

Suddenly, one more gunshot rang out and then, a second later, it was followed by a rumbling noise. However, nothing could be seen from where the children and Uti were standing.

"Maybe part of the tunnel collapsed," Sarah suggested.

Uti thought for a moment. "Yes, that might explain the rumbling noise, and there's a chance that the shots that were fired caused the rock fall."

"But what could the men have been shooting at?" Amy asked.

"I have no idea," Uti admitted.

There was silence for the next few minutes as the

children and Uti stayed where they were, wondering if there were going to be any other sounds. But there weren't.

Uti sighed. "Well, I suppose there's nothing we can do, so we may as well go back to the plane."

~

As sunset approached, Joe began to get worried. Suddenly, he thought of an idea. "Hey, what if we flew over the valley in the plane again? If we do that now, we might be able to see the men and then we would know that nothing had happened to them."

Uti nodded. "Yes, that's a good idea." He started the engine and soon the plane was climbing steadily. Once they were at the top of the mountain, he levelled out.

As they flew across the valley, everyone gazed down. There was no sign of the men. All they could see were gorillas.

"I wonder where they could be," Amy muttered anxiously.

"I'll do another pass in case we missed something," Uti said.

As the plane flew across the valley once more, the three children peered through the window.

Suddenly, Sarah saw a very large, hairy, spider crawling across the roof. Her face froze in horror as she pointed towards it. "Spider!"

Joe and Amy quickly looked up and were shocked to see the biggest spider that they had ever seen in their lives.

Uti didn't waste any time as he quickly wound down his window with one hand and, with the other, reached out to grab the spider. The spider sensed the man's intentions and scuttled away.

Joe realised that Uti could do with some help in catching the spider and, though he didn't like touching the creepy crawly, he knew he had to help since the girls were deathly afraid of spiders.

So, with the girls screaming in his ear telling him to be careful, he stood up and cupped his hands over the spider. Then, trying his utmost to keep his composure, Joe leaned across Uti and threw the spider out of the window. He breathed a sigh of relief and sat back down.

However, before everyone could smile and relax, the aircraft suddenly shuddered as a tree branch smashed into the left wing and the sound of tearing metal was heard.

With a shock, everyone realised that, while the encounter with the spider had been going on, the plane had steadily been getting lower. Thus, the inevitable had occurred. The plane had got so close to one of the tall trees that surrounded the lake that a thick branch had smashed into the wing.

As part of the wing fell to the ground below, Uti tried to stabilize the aircraft, but he couldn't. "Better hold on! It's going to be a rough landing!"

As the plane hurtled towards the ground, the children anxiously peered out of the window, wondering where they were going to crash land.

# CHAPTER 14

# ORANGE EYES

Ten seconds later, the plane zoomed down and skimmed above the grass. It got lower and lower until the wheels touched the ground.

A few moments later, there was a lurch as the aircraft slammed into something solid. Everyone lurched forward, but luckily, they were wearing seatbelts and no one was thrown through the window.

Glad that they were now on solid ground, the children quickly opened the door and climbed out. Uti quickly followed.

Joe glanced around. "So, what do we do now?"

"We need to find Captain Red and his men," Uti replied.

"But what about the dangerous animals that live in the valley?" Sarah questioned. "We don't have any weapons to protect ourselves."

"I do have a pistol in my rucksack," Uti admitted. "It's been a long time since I last used it, but I'm sure it still works. So, we…" He suddenly paused. "I might need to use it sooner than I expected."

Sarah frowned. "What do you mean?"

"Look over to your right," Uti replied.

The children did just that and saw an animal that

looked like a mixture between a dog and a wolf. However, the fur on this animal was green, so green that it was very hard to tell the animal apart from the grass. But the eyes stood out. They glowed bright orange. It was these that scared the children more than anything.

The animal gazed at them for what seemed like an eternity but, in reality, was probably only a minute or so, before it disappeared from sight.

Sarah turned to Uti. "Is that a wolf or a dog?"

"I would say it's closer to a wolf than a dog," Uti admitted. "However, as you have seen, a lot of these animals are a bit different from the animals we are familiar with. The gorillas are larger than other gorillas and have white fur, and these wolves look a bit different from wolves you may have seen pictures of. Now, we need to get a fire going immediately. Most animals are afraid of fire and, while I'm not sure if that is the case with these wolves, I hope it is."

Uti paused and peered up at the sky. "As you no doubt have noticed, the sun is setting fast. So, though I intended searching straight away, I think our best course of action would be to build a fire which will protect us from the wolves and it will also allow Will or the men to see the flames."

"But we still have time to search now," Joe argued, glancing around. "It's not dark yet."

"No, it isn't," Uti agreed. "However, we do need to gather the wood for the fire and get it roaring before that happens. So, we need to find as many dry branches as we can."

"Okay, we'll do as you say," Amy said. "Where shall we get the wood from?"

Uti glanced around. He then pointed to a number of fallen trees to the right of them. "See if you can break a few of those branches off."

As the three children made their way to the trees, Joe looked around. This valley was clearly different from the other part of the island. Much more dangerous, at least that's how it seemed. It was the unknown factor that was the scariest. What animals were out there in the darkness? Had Will encountered them? Joe had no idea. All he could do was hope that Will was safe and sound, tucked in a cave somewhere waiting for help to arrive.

The branches were fairly easy to break off and the children collected as many as they could. They dragged them over to Uti who was preparing a spot to build the fire. As their friend started to build a tee pee with the wood they had collected, he glanced up at them. "Just as I had hoped, this wood is dry."

"What about the storm we were caught in the other day?" Amy questioned. "Surely the rain fell here as well."

Uti shook his head. "Not necessarily. The storm may have died out before reaching here." He focused his attention back to the fire. "This should be enough wood to get the fire going."

The children watched on as Uti scrunched up some scraps of paper that he had gathered from inside the plane and then, taking out some matches, lit the paper.

Flames quickly spread from the paper onto the branches. Just as Joe was about to congratulate Uti, he happened to see something orange out of the corner of his eye. He glanced around and two of the brightest orange eyes beamed right at him, then another two, and then another two. Shocked, he turned to the others. "The wolves are back!"

The girls and Uti were stunned. Unbeknownst to them, while they had been talking, a large number of wolves, at least eight, had surrounded them.

The animals stood there, not making a single sound. It was as though they were waiting for something. Sarah didn't like it and she clutched Amy's hand in terror.

"Relax. It's going to be okay," Amy said. "We've got the fire going, so they aren't going to attack us."

~

Not until the fire started to burn down did Joe realise that they had a problem on their hands. They needed more wood or else the fire would die completely. However, the wolves were still standing within sight of them, not as many as before, but enough to make them scared to go and collect more wood for the fire.

Even Uti was starting to get a bit worried and, though he hadn't said anything to the children, Joe sensed this by the expression on the man's face. While the children had spent the last thirty minutes resting in the plane, Uti had been sitting by the fire, but he was now pacing back and forth.

Joe climbed out of the plane and walked over to Uti. "What are we going to do?"

"I'm not sure. We need more wood. Otherwise, the fire's going to die out. But there is no need for all of us to go." Uti walked over to the fire and foraged around until he found a piece of wood that was burning on one end and cool on the other. He picked it up. "You're in charge until I get back."

Joe nodded. "Don't be long."

"I won't." Uti slowly walked away from the fire and swept his fire torch from side to side. The wolves parted and let him through.

Joe kept his eye on the fire torch as the light slowly

got dimmer and dimmer.

There was a noise as the girls came out of the plane. "Where did Uti go?" Amy asked.

"To find some more wood," Joe replied.

"But what about the wolves?" Sarah questioned. "Won't they attack him?"

"Not with the fire torch he's holding," Joe replied. "However, I hope he comes back quickly because I doubt the fire will last too long."

## CHAPTER 15

# THE DIVERSION

Within a matter of minutes, Uti was back. He had only one branch in his hand. "This is all I could find and, with my fire torch dying, I didn't want to risk being out there any longer."

As Uti dropped the branch onto the fire, the children peered around. The wolves were now back in strength and the girls were horrified to see that, not only were they back, there were more than before. There were at least ten of them.

As they growled and snarled, the girls clutched hands. Joe turned to Uti. "What are we going to do now? That branch you brought isn't going to keep the fire going for too much longer."

Uti shook his head. "No, it isn't, which means we have to take as much stuff as we can and flee the area. The only way we're going to survive is if we head for the gorillas by the lake. Only they can save us now."

Joe frowned. "What do you mean?"

"If we lead the wolves to the path of gorillas, there's every chance the wolves will be scared off by the gorillas," Uti replied. "Then, hopefully, we'll be able to slip away."

"But what if we can't? What if the gorillas attack us?"

Sarah asked, frightened.

"It's a chance we have to take," Uti replied. "I just wish you three hadn't come along. You should have stayed with the natives. I blame myself. I shouldn't have allowed you to come."

Joe shook his head. "No, we wanted to come, and I'm still glad we did. Your plan seems like a good one. I'm sure it will work out. So, what do we need to do?"

"Grab the best fire torch you can find," Uti said. "Actually, make that two fire torches for each person, and I'll go into the plane and get some stuff together that we might need and put that into a rucksack. I'll be back in a jiffy."

Uti was true to his word for, as soon as the children had chosen their fire torches, the man had returned. He found himself a fire torch and turned to the children. "We'll head in one line towards the lake. Stay close enough so that the wolves don't think about coming between us, but not so close that your fire torch is burning the person in front of you. Is that clear?"

Joe nodded. "I'll go last to make sure the girls are safe."

Uti nodded. "Okay, let's get going then."

Without further ado, the group left the plane. As soon as the wolves realised that the group was moving on, they followed suit. However, presumably due to the fire torches, they didn't attack, but their eyes could always be seen glinting dangerously.

At first, the group walked at a steady pace, not wanting to trip over anything since evening was rapidly turning into night and the moon was glowing in the sky. Luckily, Uti had got his bearings earlier when they had crashed and knew the direction in which they had to walk in. But, as time went on and five minutes turned into ten and, one by one, the fire torches died out, Uti got worried. And, as his fire torch also died, he reached into his pocket and pulled out his torch. After switching it on, he glanced back at the others and yelled out. "Let's run!"

The wolves, as though sensing their opportunity, started to bark and growl, louder and louder. The girls were scared. They screamed out in fear and ran after Uti.

Suddenly, Uti skidded to a stop as there was a roar in front of him and the torch illuminated a massive creature. Everyone realised instantly that they had reached the gorillas.

With one last burst of energy, the children followed Uti as he ducked beneath the trees near the lake. As they did so, there was a cacophony of noise as numerous birds and animals screeched out.

It soon became clear that every animal in the area was awake and, from the noises, it seemed as though the wolves were being chased away by the gorillas. Their plan had worked.

A few moments later, they reached the edge of the lake. Fortunately, there was almost a full moon and so there was enough light to see where they were.

Uti, breathing heavily for he wasn't used to running so much, turned to the children. "Follow me and be as quiet as you can. We'll continue walking and keep as close to the shoreline of the lake as we can, but don't fall in."

The group continued, this time as silently as they could. They had only been walking for a few minutes when Uti suddenly stopped. He glanced behind them.

"What's wrong?" Joe asked.

"I think one of the wolves is following us, but I'm not sure," Uti replied. "It's a bit hard to tell."

"What should we do?" Sarah asked anxiously.

"Let's find somewhere to hide," Amy suggested.

"We could do that, but wolves normally track by smell, so I'm not sure if it would fool him." Uti swung the torch around and, once his eyes caught sight of an area thickly overgrown with bushes, he headed towards it. "This might be a good spot."

Sarah peered at the bushes that were as tall as the black man. "I hope they're not prickly."

"Getting scratched is better than being attacked by a wolf," Uti said.

The children followed Uti through the bushes and, within a matter of moments, the bushes grew less dense. It was with surprise and disbelief that the group found themselves beside a wooden hut. As the man shone the torch all around them, the children gasped, amazed that it was in such a good condition.

"This must have been built by someone who was shipwrecked here," Joe said.

Uti nodded. "Yes, that's the only explanation. I don't believe the natives would have been to this place." He opened the door and the children followed him inside.

"At least this is somewhere safe for the time being," Amy said.

"Yes," Sarah piped up. "Especially since we can close the door."

Joe glanced around, suddenly spotting something as he did so. "Look, a hole!"

## CHAPTER 16

# RESCUED!

Uti shone his torch towards the hole. "The ground must have given way there at some point."

Amy thought for a moment. "What if Will was being chased by a gorilla or wolf and came through the bushes just like us? He could have fallen down the hole since he wouldn't have had a torch."

"That is unlikely, but possible." Joe hurried over to the hole and quietly called out. "Will! Are you there?"

There was no answer.

Sarah frowned. "Why aren't you shouting? If Will is–"

"We can't shout," Uti interrupted. "Not while a wolf is possibly close by."

"Well, how long are we going to wait then?" Sarah questioned. "After all, we have no idea if a wolf is following us and, if one is, we don't know how long he will stay around."

"True," Uti admitted. "Which is why it might be best if I have a look down the hole myself." He shone the torch down the hole, examining every angle. "It's not too far down, maybe ten feet or so to the bottom. If I were to use the rope in the rucksack, I should have no problem getting down. Even if Will isn't there, it'll still be interesting to look around." Uti suddenly made up his mind and fumbled about in his rucksack. He then handed Joe the torch. "Can you shine the light on the hole while I tie the rope?"

Joe did as Uti asked while he tied one end of the rope to a post. Then, making sure it was tied on tight, he threw the rest of the rope down the hole. He then slid down the rope. Then, once he had done so, he asked Joe to throw the torch down. When the boy had done this, the man shone the torch around. "There appears to be a cavern down here. I'll check it out. Back in a minute."

The children watched from above as he disappeared from sight. They could see flashes of light as the torch was shone around the walls of the dark cavern, but that was all.

The seconds seemed to tick by awfully slowly, and then the light became brighter and then Uti appeared below them. He called out. "You were right! Will's down here."

"What? Thank goodness!" Amy exclaimed, happy beyond belief.

"Is he okay?" Sarah asked.

"He's a bit banged up," Uti admitted. "But he'll be fine once we can get him back to the other island. He's just a bit disorientated and needs some food and water and a good sleep. He has a few bruises, but I don't think he has any broken bones. I think the best way to get him out of the hole since he doesn't have the strength to climb up, is for me to tie the rope around his waist and then I'll climb up and pull him up."

Joe nodded. "That sounds like a good idea."

Uti went to work. The three children eagerly glanced down and beamed as they caught sight of their red haired friend a minute later.

Will smiled and waved his hand, but he didn't say anything. His clothes looked torn and dirty, and his face had some dirt on it. But, despite all this, he still had a cheerful expression on his face.

Before long, Uti had the rope around Will and he climbed up himself. Then, with the others helping, he pulled the rope up. As soon as Will was alongside the others, all three children hugged him.

"So, what happened to you?" Joe said.

Will sighed. "I thought if I jumped from the tree to the ledge I might be able to get down. But I couldn't. Behind the ledge was a cave and a tunnel and I went through there, and that's how I ended up in this valley."

Amy put her arms around Will. "I'm just so happy that nothing happened to you."

Will gingerly smiled. "So am I. I have to admit it was pretty scary down in that hole. I didn't think anyone would find me, and then I saw the light from a torch and hoped it was someone friendly who could get me out of there. But I never imagined it would be Uti."

"Yes, it was a surprise to us as well when…" Amy suddenly stopped speaking as a sound was heard outside the hut.

"Quiet!" Uti quickly switched off his torch.

Suddenly, the door creaked open and a light dazzled everyone. The shape moved forward and then, and only then, did everyone breathe a sigh of relief as they saw it was Lofty.

"What are you doing here?" Uti asked.

"What do you think? I was searching for you," Lofty replied. "I thought I saw a light earlier and decided to investigate. But then the light disappeared. When I saw these bushes I wondered if you had gone through them."

"Where are the others?" Amy asked.

"Back at the makeshift camp," Lofty replied.

"Which is where?" Uti asked.

"Not too far from here," Lofty replied. "We're camped by a cave up by the steep slope. When we saw your plane crash, Slim and Bones went searching for you, but they got scared and soon returned. As it began to grow dark, I realised that the only way we were going to get out of this valley was with you, and so I decided to go searching for you by myself."

"Okay, let's get to your camp without delay," Uti said.

"Yes, and let's hope we don't meet any wolves." Lofty suddenly caught sight of Will. "Hey, I see you found the boy."

Uti nodded. "Yes, he'd fallen down a hole. How far did you say your camp was?"

Lofty thought for a moment. "Oh, I would say a twenty minute walk."

Uti looked at Will. "Do you think you can walk that far?"

"I'm not sure," Will admitted.

"I'll help you," Joe said.

"And so will I," Sarah piped up.

"Me too," Amy said.

Will smiled. "Thanks. If my legs get a bit weary, I'll let you know."

## CHAPTER 17

# WHAT DO WE DO NOW?

Twenty minutes later, the group arrived at the cave where the four men were lounging about.

Captain Red smiled as he saw Will. "There you are, lad."

Will nodded. "A bit sore here and there, but it could have been—"

"Come on," Uti interrupted, pulling the red haired boy over to the fire. "Let's get you warm."

As Will settled down next to the campfire and was handed some food and water, Uti turned to Captain Red. "So, what's been going on since we last saw you?"

The man grimly smiled. "We encountered vampire bats in the tunnel."

"Vampire bats?" Amy questioned, bewildered.

Captain Red nodded. "Bats that eat blood. They mostly feast on mammals, but they can also attack humans. These bats weren't exactly like the ones I encountered last summer, but not in a good way. These seemed more blood thirsty."

"I can't say I've had the pleasure of meeting those bats," Uti admitted. "However, I've heard that they can be dangerous to humans, especially if they're starving."

"Which we found out the hard way," Captain Red

complained. "As my men started getting bitten, we started shooting. Not really in the hope of killing the animals, but causing a distraction, which is why we shot at the stalactites. As they crashed down, we ran away. It was lucky we did since we had only been running for a few minutes before a huge pile of rocks fell down behind and—"

"So the tunnel is now blocked?" Uti interrupted.

Captain Red nodded. "We had no choice but to continue on. When we arrived at the cave, we encountered a group of wolves feasting on a dead animal. As they came towards us, we scared them away by shooting at them. However, since we didn't have much ammunition left, we decided it was best to sit still until you came looking for us."

"So, how do you reckon we can get out of this mess?" Bones questioned. "Can your plane be fixed up?"

Uti thought for a moment. "It's possible, but it's also possible that, by the time we get back to the plane, the wheels will have sunk too deep into the mud. You see, there are a lot of places on this island that are boggy."

"But how else are we going to get out of here?" Captain Red asked.

"Well, we could find another tunnel or we could try to unblock the one you came through," Uti replied.

"I'm telling you, there's no way to unblock it," Slim said. "And, even if we did unblock it, then we'd have to face those bats again and, well, I've seen many creatures in my lifetime but they're one type of creature you don't want to mess with, especially if you don't have any weapons."

"Well, I think it's best we try to reopen the tunnel," Uti stated. "But there's no need for the children to come."

Captain Red nodded and turned to Bones. "You can

stay with the kids."

"Good luck," Will said.

A minute later, the group departed, leaving the thin man and the four children by the fire.

They were gone for so long that the children wondered if something had happened to them. Then, after two hours had elapsed, they returned. All of them looked exhausted and worn out. They collapsed to the ground beside the fire. Even Uti looked dirty and worn out.

"So, how did it go?" Joe asked.

"Well, we moved some rocks," Uti replied. "But who knows how many are still on the other side? Since our torchlight was getting low, we decided to head back." He turned to Will. "How did you manage to survive the bats?"

"I had no problem with them," Will stated. "In fact, I didn't even know the bats were there. Maybe it was because it was so dark. I just walked slowly and I kept my hands up against the wall. There was one time when the wall disappeared and there seemed to be a cave of some sort. Now that I think about it, I did notice a distinct smell in that area. I just supposed some animal had died or something. Since I had no wall to guide me, I just walked slowly with my hands out in front of me and went straight ahead until I came in contact with the wall again."

Uti nodded. "That's interesting."

"Maybe the bats didn't attack Will because they didn't know he was there since he didn't have a torch and he wasn't making much noise," Amy suggested.

"Yes, I would say that could be the case. Which means, if we were to go down the tunnel, we could do what Will did. But, maybe the plane is the best option now, because we could be moving rocks for some time and still not get through." Uti glanced around the group. "It's fairly late now, so I say we all get some rest. Just make sure enough wood is put on the fire because we don't want any unwelcome visitors during the night."

Captain Red nodded. "That's one good thing about this area. There's an old, dead tree nearby which is where we got the firewood from, and there's plenty more there. I'll go and get some more now."

Everyone collected armfuls of sticks and branches and, after that was done, preparations were made to go to sleep. But, before Joe did so, he turned to Will. "You probably know this, but I'm really glad you're back with us."

Will nodded. "So am I. I was thinking about you and the girls all the time and I knew you would be searching for me, which is why I still had hope someone would find me. If I'd been on the island all alone, things might have been different."

Joe nodded. "Yes, well, now at least we're back together again."

"But we're still not out of the valley," Sarah piped up.

"No, we're not," Joe admitted. "We might be stranded, but at least we're all together again."

## CHAPTER 18

# GOOD AND BAD NEWS

The children tossed and turned throughout the night. It seemed as though whenever they were close to falling asleep, a cry from an animal rang out. It was either a howl, squawk or growl, which made the children sit up and glance around. Also, the rocky floor of the cave was quite uncomfortable to sleep on. The grass would have been nicer, but that was away from the safety of the fire and, as much as the children wanted to sleep, they also wanted to be safe.

As dawn broke and tinges of pink could be seen in the sky, the children were glad that the night was over. There wasn't much to have for breakfast, just a few snacks that Uti had brought from the plane as part of the emergency supplies.

Joe wondered what they were going to do when the supplies were all gone, but he felt sure they'd soon find a way out of the valley. Hearing a noise, he stood up and glanced around. As a helicopter came into view a few seconds later at the far end of the valley, he smiled. He didn't know how or why, but help was at hand.

As the craft flew closer, and a rainbow star on a blue background became visible on the tail section, Uti frowned. "That looks like the helicopter I sold to

Grace."

"Grace? Who is she?" Captain Red questioned.

"A zoologist who is doing some research on Oxley Island," Uti replied. "We were visiting her the night my cabin cruiser was torn from its moorings. Quick now, we need to do everything we can to attract her attention."

The group ran from the cave, waving frantically while the men used up the rest of the ammunition in the hope that the noise of the shots would be heard above the sound of the helicopter as it flew overhead.

Everyone was glad when the helicopter changed course and flew in their direction. Shortly, a hand appeared and waved down at them.

It wasn't long before the helicopter landed on the nearest patch of flat ground and, as it did so, Uti caught sight of the pilot. It was Grace. "What are you doing here?"

The woman smiled as she stepped out of the aircraft, her long red hair blowing to and fro as she walked over to the group. "I was worried, and a good thing I was. I saw your crashed plane at the other end of the valley."

"How did you know where to find us?" Uti asked.

"I just searched in every direction," Grace replied. "But I was lucky. I was almost ready to head home when I saw these two islands."

"What about fuel?" Captain Red asked. "Do you have enough to reach the island you set out from?"

"I believe so. I did bring a spare can, so I'll fill up the tank before I set off again. Speaking of which..." Grace paused as she glanced around at the group. "I don't think everyone can fit in the helicopter."

"What do you mean?" Lofty asked.

"Well, this helicopter isn't designed for more than six people at a time," Grace replied.

Uti nodded. "Yes, that's right, and we shouldn't try to squeeze everyone in, since this helicopter is quite old and not in the best condition. So, I think we need to split into two groups. The children can go first, and then—"

"Hold on a minute," Captain Red snarled as he quickly drew out his pistol. "I've still got a bullet or two left in this, so you'd better listen to what I have to say."

"What's going on?" Grace asked, glancing towards Uti.

"Just listen to me, young lady," Captain Red stated. "My friends and I are going first. You're going to take me away from this island and then, when we're safe and sound, you can come back and pick up everyone else."

"But what if some dangerous animal comes—" Amy said.

"I agreed to help Uti search for a missing kid and that's what I've done," Captain Red interrupted. Now it's time for me to get off this island and, if you refuse to fly this helicopter, then I'll have to fly it myself."

"You can't just leave us here," Sarah piped up, suddenly realising what was about to happen.

"We can and we will," Captain Red stated.

"But we had a deal," Joe argued. "You would help us find Will in exchange for Uti saving your life."

Captain Red laughed. "Yes, which I did. But what if you lot flew off now and then, by the time my men get back to civilization, the area was swarming with police officers?" He shook his head. "There's no way that's going to happen."

Uti glared at Captain Red. "If you do anything to harm Grace, the police will be the least of your worries."

Captain Red laughed. "Relax. I just need her to fly me out of here. I can do many things, but piloting a helicopter isn't something I have ever done. But there's always a first time. However, if I happen to crash, then who's going to pick you up?"

"Okay, I'll take you back," Grace offered.

Captain Red nodded. "Good girl. Now, let's get the helicopter refuelled."

After this was done, the escaped prisoners climbed aboard the helicopter. As the aircraft rose up into the sky, the children looked on. All were silent. None of them could think of anything useful to say. They had never expected anything like this to happen and didn't know what to think or say. One moment they thought they had been rescued and now, just five or so minutes later, they were back where they started.

## CHAPTER 19

# THE WAITING GAME

Seeing the glum look on their faces, Uti smiled at them. "Don't you worry. Grace will be back here in no time at all. Let's just go and sit back by the fire and await her return."

The children slowly walked back to the fire and sat down. Just before the woman had left, she had mentioned that she hoped to be back within two hours. However, as the two hour mark came and went, and still no sign of the helicopter was seen or heard, the children started to get concerned.

Uti, wanting to cheer them up, decided to tell them a story about when he flew to South America with a friend and got lost in the wilderness. It was a very exciting story and the children did their best to concentrate. However, they kept on glancing up at the sky, wondering when Grace would return.

Since the woman had not returned by the time Uti had finished his tale, he started telling them about another trip that he had gone on, this time to an ancient Mayan temple. Even though the story was exciting, none of the children could keep their full attention on it.

As two hours turned into three, Joe realised that

something needed to be said. "She's not coming back, is she?"

Uti shook his head. "She'll return, mark my words. You can count on it. There's no way she's going to leave us stranded here."

"But she should have been back by now!" Sarah exclaimed, letting her emotions get the better of her.

Joe turned to Uti. "What do you think has happened?"

Uti thought for a moment. "Well, I would say that it took longer than Grace imagined it would to fly back to Oxley Island."

"I suppose so," Will muttered.

Everyone fell silent and, for the next hour or two, the only action was making sure that the fire had enough wood to keep it burning. None of the group had seen any sign of animals so far this morning, which was a good thing.

As the morning turned into afternoon, Uti suddenly stood up. "I think it might be a good idea to make our way to the crashed plane just to see if we could fly out."

Joe nodded. "I suppose we might as well have a look at the plane. There's no need to sit here all the time doing nothing."

"But what about the wolves and gorillas?" Amy questioned. "What if they come across us while we're walking to the plane?"

"Well, if we stay close to the outer edge of the valley and just walk beside the steep part we'd be away from the gorillas, and the wolves might not be out at this time of day, so we should be fine," Uti replied.

~

By the time Uti and the four children reached the

plane, two hours had elapsed. Fortunately, though, no animals had been spotted. Unfortunately, they still hadn't seen any sign of the helicopter.

Once they reached the plane, it only took one look at the undercarriage of the aircraft to discover that it was hopeless. The wheels could now no longer be seen. The ground had swallowed them up.

Uti knelt down and examined the ground. "Just as I feared. There's no way we're going to move this plane."

"So, what now?" Amy asked.

"Well, I will have another look in the plane to see if there's something we can use," Uti replied as he made his way to the cabin door.

The children also searched. The only useful item that they found was a small emergency kit which had some matches, a flare gun, and a map. The map was not very useful since it was just a general map of the Caribbean, but Uti wanted to bring everything along because he thought the piece of paper would help start a fire if they had to make one.

After these things were in the rucksack, Uti turned to the children. "I say we rest here for a bit and then, if we don't see any sign of the helicopter in an hour or so, we return back to the cave."

"But what's the point of going back to the cave?" Will questioned.

"Especially since the tunnel is blocked up," Sarah pointed out.

Uti nodded. "We need to go back because when Grace returns that will be the place the helicopter will land. Besides, even though the tunnel is blocked, if the situation gets worse, we could attempt to move some more rocks and see if we could make a hole."

Amy nodded. "But if you and the other men couldn't move them, what chance do we have?"

"We did move a few," Uti admitted. "For all we know, there could just be two rocks standing between us and a way out."

Joe nodded. "I suppose it's better to go back there and try to see if we can get to the tunnel."

"But what about the bats that the men saw?" Sarah questioned.

"Well, I didn't encounter any bats," Will pointed out. "So maybe we can do what I did."

"We can decide what to do when we reach that part," Uti said. "Right now though, let's have a rest. I'm sure your legs must be a bit weary."

Sarah nodded. "Yes, it'll be good to have a rest."

## CHAPTER 20

# STILL MORE WAITING

For the next hour or so, they rested. And, when there was still no sign of the helicopter, they made their way back to the cave. There they waited until evening approached.

Uti sighed. "I really can't understand it. Grace should have been back by now. I still think she's going to come but, just in case, we should prepare for the worst. So, let's see if we can move some of the rocks."

"But what if the helicopter comes while we are in the tunnel?" Amy pointed out.

"Well, we'll have to leave someone here on guard," Uti replied.

Will raised his hand. "I'll stay. I'm still not feeling the best, so I'm not sure if I'd be that much help."

"Yes, that makes sense," Uti replied. "If you do see any sign of the helicopter, yell out and wave."

Will nodded. "I'll do that, and good luck."

Without any further delay, the rest of the party made their way down the tunnel. Unfortunately, the torch that Uti had was slowly dying and thus, he realised they couldn't stay in the tunnel for too long since they needed light to move the rocks.

After handing the torch over to Sarah, Uti reached

for a small rock. "Let's just concentrate on the small rocks for the time being. Maybe that will work."

And so, they began to remove one small rock after another. After a short while, they made a hole, but then, just as quickly as it had appeared, it disappeared since the rocks above the hole collapsed and fell into it. Not wanting to abandon their mission, the group continued, pulling out one rock after another. But, as time passed and the torchlight got dimmer and dimmer, Uti realised they had to stop. Otherwise, their wouldn't be enough light for them to find their way back to Will.

"Well, I suppose this isn't going to work." Uti stood up and, after wiping the dust and dirt off his hands, took the torch from Sarah. "Okay, let's head back to Will."

Once they had returned to the cave, they found Will where they had left him, sitting on one of the rocks, gazing up at the sky. As he heard them, he glanced around. No words needed to be spoken as it was evident by Will's expression that the helicopter hadn't arrived.

However, the one thing that had changed was the weather. The sun was on its way down. Darkness was approaching.

"Well, it looks as though we'll be staying another night here," Uti stated. "Come on, let's get some dry wood for the fire."

Thankful that it hadn't yet rained for that would really spoil their chance of making a fire, everyone did their part and managed to get some dry wood. Then, using the map and the matches that they had got from the emergency kit in the plane, Uti attempted to start the fire.

Unfortunately, it was harder than it looked and

quite a few matches were wasted before a few flames appeared. Maybe it was because the piece of paper wasn't as dry as it should have been or maybe the wood was a bit damp but, either way, they definitely had trouble starting a fire.

Upon looking up at the sky, the children saw that the weather had indeed changed. Dark clouds were scudding across the sky and, off in the distance, thunder rumbled. It looked as though a storm was approaching, but would it just bring wind or would it bring wind and rain?

The children didn't know and, as the minutes passed and Uti began to get worried, he turned towards the children. "I'm afraid I can't start the fire. While there's matches left, I've used up all of the paper."

"But what are we going to do to keep the animals at bay if we don't have fire?" Sarah questioned.

Uti sighed. He looked towards the cave entrance and glanced out. "I think..." He suddenly paused. Wondering what was going on, the children joined him by the cave entrance and peered down, seeing straight away what had caught his attention.

A wolf.

Terror took hold of them. One wolf they could deal with, but it was likely that the wolf would soon be joined by his companions. Then they would be in trouble.

"We need to think of a plan," Uti stated. "Without any fire and without any weapons, we're defenceless against the wolves."

"What about the flare gun?" Joe suggested.

"That's only good for a very short period of time," Uti replied. "And I would prefer to keep that for an emergency. I just wish I knew what had happened to Grace. If I knew for certain she wasn't coming—"

"I'm sure she'll come," Joe interrupted. "But, I think we need to admit that we're going to be on our own tonight. It's not dark yet, but it soon will be and, once darkness arrives, it's going to be harder to move about. So, whatever we're going to do, I say we do it now."

Uti suddenly stood up. "I have an idea. I don't think it will work, but let's try one final time to move the rocks."

"But we tried that and it was useless," Amy argued. "Every time we opened up a small hole, more rocks fell down and filled it up."

Uti nodded. "Yes, but what if, as soon as a little gap was opened, one of us went into it?"

"I think I see what you mean," Joe said. "Let's try it. It's not as though we have anything to lose."

"I'll come too, then," Will said. "I don't think Grace is going to arrive tonight and, if we only have one final chance of getting the hole open, we all need to go."

The group hurried down the tunnel. By the time they reached the rock fall, the torchlight was very dim, so dim they could hardly see. But, despite this, the children went to work and, as Uti had suggested, as soon as a little gap had opened, Uti put his feet into the gap and, miraculously, it worked. Soon, his feet were dangling on the other side. Unfortunately, by now, the torchlight had completely faded away, and Sarah, who now had the box of matches, was striking a match every now and then.

As soon as Uti was able to make his way through the little hole, the children followed suit, making sure to keep close together and thus not giving the rocks any chance to fall down into the gap. Will was the last to go and, as he did so, the rocks crumbled behind him and, as the others pulled his legs out of the gap, more rocks fell upon the hole, quickly closing it up.

Due to the torch no longer working, the four children held hands while Uti lit a match every now and then just to make sure that they were on the right track and that the path up ahead was flat.

~

After they had been walking for nearly fifteen minutes, they came to a big cave. Straight away, a strange smell drifted into the nostrils of the group. Something living, or dead, was causing this new smell.

Only one thought ran through Joe's head. He hoped he was mistaken, but he was pretty sure they had arrived at the cave with the bats.

Uti used up the last of the matches to see around the cave, and he and the children realised that things were not good. The cave was a fairly big one and was filled with stalagmites and stalactites and, hanging from the walls, masses of bats. They were double the size of a normal bat and were completely black, all except for their eyes which glowed bright yellow.

## CHAPTER 21

# VAMPIRE BATS

The only good thing about this cave was that, at the other end, a glimmer of light could be seen. That was the end of the tunnel. Once they got there they would be on the ledge and, from there, they could use the rope to climb down. And, even though they were still going to have to trek through the jungle and then somehow find a way to travel to the other island, at least they would be out of the valley. However, they first had to deal with the bats.

"Let's think what we're going to do," Uti said as he retreated down the tunnel for a few feet before sitting down. "Do we go slow or do we go fast? Do we go quiet? Do we go noisy? These are all things we need to think about."

Will nodded. "Well, I went slow and quiet, so I say we should do that."

"But there was only one of you and now there are five of us," Sarah piped up. "Now they might be more alert."

"Well, it's a risk either way," Amy said. "We could start off slow and quiet and then, if we see that they're taking notice, we could make a run for it. Once we reach the tunnel, we ought to be safe. I don't think they'll come after us in broad daylight."

"No, but it is getting dark outside," Uti stated. "So, the longer we wait, the more likely it is they'll pursue us since these creatures see better in the dark than we do. Of course, now that our torch isn't working and we're out of matches, we don't have any choice but to go slowly."

"We still have the flare gun," Will pointed out.

Uti nodded. "Yes, we do. I'm going to hold on to it and keep it close at hand in case we need it. Well, let's get going, shall we?"

"Yes, let's get this over with," Sarah said.

The group made their way back into the cave. Slowly and surely, using the light up ahead, the group walked across the cave. Fortunately, there weren't any stalactites or stalagmites near the middle of the cave and thus, all they had to do was walk in a straight line and they would be safe. However, since they wanted to be as quiet as possible, they had to walk very slowly indeed. Since the cave was a large one, Uti estimated it was going to take five or so minutes for them to cross the width of it.

They were around halfway through when the situation went from good to bad. Suddenly, out of nowhere, Amy sneezed. She had tried to hold the sneeze in, but she just couldn't do it. As the sound echoed throughout the cave, the few yellow eyes became more and more until there were more than a hundred yellow eyes peering at them. Uti didn't wait any longer. "Run!"

As he did so, he took hold of the flare gun and fired it directly to the right and a bit up. The flare shot out of the gun and slammed straight into one of the stalactites. As it crashed upon the cave floor, it sent another stalactite, which was next to it, also to the ground. Before long, the cave was abuzz with the flapping of wings as the creatures attempted to fly away from the destruction that was being caused and swarmed towards the cave entrance.

The children and Uti had somewhat of a lead to start with, but the gap narrowed and narrowed with every passing second. Even though the children ran as fast as they could, the gap between them and the bats got closer and closer. The light became brighter and brighter as they reached the end of the tunnel, and then suddenly, they were out on the ledge. Uti ran straight for the rope, knowing that they couldn't stay on the ledge with the bats behind them. "Quick, down the rope as fast as you can!"

As the girls started to go down the rope, Uti turned to face the bats. He had no weapons left. All he had was his hands and he waved them to and fro, trying to make the bats go away. The boys followed suit for a few seconds before joining the girls.

A few of the bats flew close to the children but, luckily, they didn't try to attack them. Joe didn't know what he would have done if one had landed on his head, but that didn't happen and, as soon as he reached the ground, he sprinted to the nearest bush.

Even though it was covered in prickles, he forced himself to lie underneath it, the others doing the same as him. They stayed like that for two or so minutes and then they stood up and looked around.

Joe sighed. "Phew, that was close."

"Yes, it was," Amy said.

"At least they didn't attack us," Will stated.

Uti nodded. "Yes, things could have ended badly if that had happened."

Suddenly, they heard a noise in the sky. It was the noise of a helicopter. Joe ran out into the open area and glanced up. He smiled with delight as he saw the aircraft flying towards him. He waved and jumped up and down in delight, hoping that Grace would see them.

Luckily she did and, within a minute, she had landed right beside them. Immediately, Uti went up to the open window and glanced anxiously at the woman. "What happened?"

"It's a long story," Grace said. "I'll tell you about it later. Just let's get going. The helicopter was making some weird noises on the flight over, so the sooner we get away from here, the better I'll feel."

Uti nodded. "Okay. You heard what she said. All aboard."

The children obeyed him without any question for they were as eager to get off this particular island as he was and, as the helicopter rose up into the sky, the children breathed a sigh of relief. They were finally safe from everything.

Joe was just about to say something when suddenly, without any warning, there was a noise and the helicopter shuddered. A few seconds later, it started to spin out of control.

Joe glanced backwards and he saw what looked to be a bat falling down towards the ground. It only took a second for him to realise what had happened. The animal had obviously made contact with the rear of the helicopter and now, not only was the creature severely injured or dead, but they were in serious trouble.

Grace tried to regain control of the helicopter, but she couldn't, and the aircraft hurtled towards the ground.

"Hold on!" Uti yelled.

The children clung to one another as the aircraft

smashed into the jungle below. Thankfully, they just missed a large tree, but the rotor blades weren't so lucky and they broke in two.

As silence reigned, the children, as well as Grace and Uti were in shock. They couldn't believe what had just happened. One moment they thought they were safe and sound and then, the next moment, they weren't.

"Was that a bat?" Grace questioned.

Uti nodded. "Yes, it was. It may have been two, actually, flying side by side. All I know is, this helicopter definitely won't be flying ever again. We'll have to walk now."

"But how are we going to get to the other island?" Amy questioned.

"Well, maybe some of the natives will find us. Anyway, if we make our way to the cove, we'll be in sight of the other island." Uti thought for a moment. "I suppose that's the best..." He suddenly and hurriedly got out of his seat, pushed open the door, and climbed out. As he examined the front of the helicopter, a worried crease came over his brow. "The fuel is leaking out."

"So? What does—" Amy asked.

"It means it could explode at any second," Uti interrupted. "We need to get out of this helicopter immediately!"

The children obeyed without question and began to make their way through the bushes towards the open clearing. Only a few seconds had passed before there was a massive roar and the helicopter exploded in a ball of flame.

Everyone was thrown to the ground.

# CHAPTER 22

## SMOKE!

The next thing Joe knew was that there was a strange smell in the air. As he groggily sat up and peered around, he realised that the situation had gone from bad to worse. He knew he had been unconscious, but he didn't know for how long. But, whatever the amount of time, it had been far too long.

There was a strong smell of smoke in the air and flames in almost every direction as bush after bush became alight. The big tree that had been right next to the helicopter was completely ablaze.

As Joe glanced around, he saw Will and his sisters slowly getting to their feet as well, but he couldn't see any sign of Uti or, for that matter, Grace. Probably because they had been closer to the aircraft when it had exploded.

Together, the children searched the bushes for them and finally came across the two of them laying side by side. They were so still, they almost looked as though they were dead.

Joe prayed that they weren't, but it was an anxious few seconds as he examined their pulses. Fortunately, they were only unconscious.

"Quick, drag them to safety!" Joe yelled. He had to

yell because now the roar of the flames had grown so loud that it was impossible to speak normally, especially when they were so close to the actual flames themselves.

It was hard work dragging Uti to safety but, luckily, as they did so and went back to find Grace, she stumbled to her feet. As she gazed around, wondering where Uti was, Joe quickly told her. Thankful that her friend was okay, she hurried over to him. Within a matter of seconds, he was also awake and, as the small group sat side by side, they realised time was running out. Thick smoke surrounded them on all sides, thus causing everyone to cough.

Luckily though, since there had been a patch of grass near them, which coincidentally was the patch of grass that Uti had landed the plane on earlier, the fire had gone around them.

Uti coughed. "It might be best to stay here and wait it out."

"We'll suffocate if we stay here!" Grace shouted. "The smoke is too unbearable. We'll probably be unconscious soon because we won't be able to breathe and that will be the end of us. We have to make a run for it."

"But where can we head?" Amy questioned. "There's jungle all around us."

"We should head for the water," Joe suggested. "That's the only place that the fire isn't going to be."

"You're right. From what I recall, the water is in that direction." Uti pointed to the left of them. Luckily, it was the area that seemed to have the least fire activity. "Now, let's stay together. In fact, let's be so close that we're almost holding hands. We can't stop for any reason, so we can't afford for anyone to split up from the group, understand?"

Will nodded. "Okay, let's just hurry."

Without delay, the group hurried in the direction in which Uti had pointed. By now, darkness had fully engulfed the area. The moon was not yet up, but storm clouds hung overhead and thunder rumbled in the distance. Every now and then, lightning flashed across the sky.

Joe prayed there would be a burst of rain, even just for a few minutes, just something to stop the fire. But, there wasn't. The only good thing about the fire was that it allowed them to see where they were heading since it was now dark. And, since they had no torch, if it hadn't been for the fire, they would have been unable to see which direction they were going in.

As the seconds ticked by, the children became more exhausted. It was one thing running through the jungle when they were not exhausted, but they had already spent the previous few hours escaping from the valley.

The worst part about the fire was the thick, black smoke. It seemed to hang about in the air, blocking out everything else. It made breathing difficult, thus it made them feel more exhausted and it was a lot harder to run.

"How far do we have to go?" Sarah asked, breathless, coughing once, and then again a few seconds later. "I don't think I can go on for much longer."

"I believe it's just up ahead," Uti promised.

He was true to his word as, half a minute or so later, the jungle parted to reveal a stretch of water. Now, all that lay between them and the water was a patch of grass and, though fire burned to the left and right of them, it wasn't making much progress across the grass, probably since it was fairly short. Thankful that this was the case, the group, now with renewed vigour, hurried in the direction of the water.

A few seconds later, the unthinkable happened as a massive tree toppled over and smashed onto the grass directly ahead of them. The tree was covered in flames and, as the branches fell against the grass and that caught alight, the party ground to a halt.

The way ahead was blocked, there was no way that they could get past the burning tree. They couldn't leap over it for it would be too high, and they couldn't go under it because there wasn't enough space.

Sarah couldn't take it anymore and she began sobbing, overwhelmed with emotions. "We're trapped, completely trapped!"

Even though Amy wanted to reassure her, she didn't, for she didn't know what to say. There were flames burning in front of them, to the left and right of them and, glancing backwards, she saw that flames now also burned behind them. They were caught in a square and the square was getting smaller with every passing second. They were trapped, just like her sister had said.

# CHAPTER 23

# RUNNING THROUGH FIRE

Even Uti, who wasn't one to admit defeat very easily, had nothing to suggest.

"Maybe if we take a running leap, we could jump over the burning tree," Sarah piped up.

Uti shook his head. "I don't think so."

"But we can't just stand here and do nothing!" Amy yelled, desperate to do something, even if the chance of success was unlikely.

"We have to do something," Joe argued. "Look, how about we run through the flames that are behind us? Those flames don't look very tall."

Uti examined the flames and thought for a moment and, as he thought, the square continued to get smaller and smaller. He then suddenly made up his mind. "Yes, the only chance we have is to run through the flames that are behind us. Cover your face with your hands as we run."

The children nodded and then, without further ado because there was no time to waste, the group turned around and raced as fast as their legs could take them towards the flames.

It seemed like madness to Will and maybe it was, but it was the only chance of survival, which is why they took it and, as they reached the flames, they leapt as high up as their legs could carry them and then they tumbled down into the grass below.

As they noticed flames that had caught fire to their clothes, they rolled back and forth along the ground until they were squashed out. Since the air was thick with smoke, they coughed every few seconds.

The group attempted to stand up and make their way away from the flames, but they couldn't. The smoke was just too overwhelming and, as soon as they got to their feet, they had to fall back down again, coughing over and over.

Joe desperately tried to pull his sisters and Will away from the flames, but he couldn't. He just didn't have the energy. The smoke was just too much. The smoke had finally caught up with him and filled his lungs to the brim. With an anguished cry, he tumbled to the grass.

As Joe's eyes began to close, a single thought tore through his mind. He was going to die. Right here, right now, and there was nothing he could do about it.

~

The next thing Joe heard was a voice close by. But where was the voice coming from? And why couldn't he understand what the voice was saying? He was hearing a strange language. And what was hitting his face?

He gathered his energy to open his eyes and, as he did so, he saw the water droplets heading directly for him. It was raining. As he sat up and glanced around, he saw that the smoke had died down and the voices belonged to the natives who were helping the others to their feet. As one came over to him, he smiled and reached his hand out. The native helped him stand up and guided him towards where he assumed the water was. As he did so, he looked up and around.

The rain was now pouring down and most of the flames had died out. Joe realised that he and the others had been very fortunate. The rain had come just in time.

He had no idea how the natives had found them, but he didn't care. He was just glad he was alive. He hoped everyone was unhurt and, as he reached the water and caught sight of Amy and Sarah sitting side by side, he smiled. He was so thankful for this second chance.

As he hugged them, he realised what being alive felt like. Even though he still liked adventures, there was no way he wanted to be put in a situation like that ever again. He and the others had been close to death, closer than they had ever been before, and he was just thankful that he was alive.

A few moments later, Will joined them, and then out of the corner of his eye, he saw Grace and Uti walking towards them. He smiled. Everyone was going to be okay.

~

As the sun crept above the horizon the following morning, Joe yawned and climbed out of bed. It hadn't been too comfy, not like the bed in Rose Cottage, for this bed was just made of branches and moss. But, he had been so worn out, that he would have been happy with any bed.

The others were also just waking up and, as he stretched, he began to smell something. Breakfast was cooking. He had no idea what it was, but it was food. And, as his stomach gurgled, he realised he hadn't eaten for some time, and boy, was he hungry.

The others were also hungry, so the four of them made their way out of the hut. It seemed as though all the natives were up and about. Most of them had congregated near the breakfast pot.

Joe then saw that Uti was standing by the shore, gazing out at the sunrise. "I'll join you in a minute. I'll just quickly go and have a talk with Uti."

Upon hearing footsteps a few moments later, Uti turned around and smiled. He put his arm around the boy. "I'd never have forgiven myself if something had happened to you last night. I shouldn't have involved you in the expedition at all. That's the closest I've ever been to feeling that my life was over."

Joe nodded. "Yes, that was as close to death as I want to be. Hey, did you find out why Grace didn't come back earlier?"

Uti nodded. "Yes. Captain Red didn't want to be taken to Oxley Island, he wanted one that had a good harbour so that he could steal another boat. So that took a while. And then, after she landed, she had to refuel again."

Joe nodded. "I expect Captain Red is far away by now."

Uti nodded. "Yes, there's nothing we can do about him, but at least we're safe. That's all that matters. Now, changing subjects, are you hungry?"

Joe nodded. "Yes, I'm starving, actually."

Uti smiled. "Then let's get something into that stomach of yours."

~

As the children splashed about in the pool at the hotel in Puerto Rosa a few days later, Mr and Mrs Mitchell lounged about in deckchairs.

Even though their parents had been worried sick about them, now that all the explanations had been given and promises to never do anything like that again, it was one big happy group.

Since Mr Mitchell had made reservations at a Spanish restaurant that evening, it wasn't long before the children climbed out of the pool.

"So, did you like this adventure better than the last one?" Joe asked.

Sarah shook her head. "Even though I wanted to see some rare animals, I didn't like the snakes, bats, lizards, wolves, and big gorillas."

Will grinned. "We certainly came across some rather unusual animals."

"I liked the orange monkeys," Amy said.

"Me too," Sarah piped up. "I hope no one locks them up in zoos."

"I agree. Animals don't belong in zoos. If anyone wants to see animals, they should see them the way we did. Well, maybe not exactly the way we did," Joe confessed. "But, that being said, I wouldn't say no to another trip to the Caribbean."

Will laughed. "No, neither would I."

Made in the USA
Monee, IL
27 February 2025